The Fish Hawk's Nest

other books by Stephen W. Meader

THE BLACK BUCCANEER

DOWN THE BIG RIVER

LONGSHANKS

RED HORSE HILL

AWAY TO SEA

KING OF THE HILLS

LUMBERJACK

THE WILL TO WIN AND OTHER STORIES

WHO RIDES IN THE DARK?

T-MODEL TOMMY

BAT

BOY WITH A PACK

CLEAR FOR ACTION

BLUEBERRY MOUNTAIN

SHADOW IN THE PINES

THE SEA SNAKE

THE LONG TRAINS ROLL

SKIPPY'S FAMILY

JONATHAN GOES WEST

BEHIND THE RANGES

RIVER OF THE WOLVES

CEDAR'S BOY

WHALER 'ROUND THE HORN

BULLDOZER

STEPHEN W. MEADER

The Fish Hawk's Nest

Illustrated by Edward Shenton

SOUTHERN SKIES

ISBN 978-1-931177-64-1 cloth
ISBN 978-1-931177- 65-8 paperback

Library of Congress Catalog Card Number 52-10065

SOUTHERN SKIES

LITTLE ROCK, ARKANSAS

www.southernskies.com

Dedication

***The republication of this book is dedicated to Bob Ocken---
true photographic artist who teaches me to see with new eyes---
by his friend, Jerry Atchley.***

FOREWORD

I discovered Cape May County, New Jersey, when I was eighteen. In my sophomore year at Haverford College, Jesse Ludlam was my roommate. My own state of New Hampshire was a long way off, and at Thanksgiving time Jess invited me to his home in Cape May Court House. Out of that four-day visit grew a lifetime of pleasant associations.

On Thanksgiving morning we wanted to build up an appetite for dinner, and we walked the four miles to Stone Harbor, on Seven Mile Beach. The wide, gray marsh, the tidal creeks, and finally the magnificent stretch of sand along the sea won my heart completely. Some day, I must have resolved even then, I would have a place of my own within the sound of that booming surf.

In the years that have passed since that day, our

family has spent many summers on the beaches of Cape May County, and we now have a cottage in Stone Harbor. But we have learned that there is more to the region than sand and sun, fishing and sailing. The farms and villages and woodland that form the backbone of the peninsula have a character all their own.

The families who settled the county more than two and a half centuries ago were sturdy stock. Their names are still dominant in Upper, Middle and Lower Townships. You will find Ludlams, Hands, Swains, Corsons, Leamings and Townsends wherever you go in that southernmost tip of New Jersey.

Like the people, there is a quaint individuality in the land itself. Nowhere else will you see such rows of gnarled old cedars lining the country roads, nor such jungles of holly in the woods. Also, to the best of my knowledge, this is the only place in the world where farmers set up poles and platforms on which fish hawks may build their nests.

With its long coast line and its maze of tidal creeks, Cape May County has been a tempting target for smugglers for two hundred years. It was as true in the prohibition days of the nineteen-twenties as in the era of high tariffs a century earlier.

For help in gathering details for this story I am indebted to three friends of long standing. They are Jesse Ludlam, my college classmate and one of South Jersey's leading citizens; Miss Sarah Thomas, revered Cape May County Librarian; and Kensil Bell, writer of boys' books and authority on the history of the Coast Guard and the Revenue Cutter Service. To each of them, my thanks.

S.W.M.

The Fish Hawk's Nest

CHAPTER I

IT WAS AFTER SUNSET when the Corson family got up from the supper table. Mrs. Corson, plump and bustling, urged the two girls to clear away the dishes. "Come, Elvira, come, Becky," she called. "Let's get things washed up while the water's still hot."

Jeremiah Corson, the father, big and bearded,

stretched his arms and went outside, followed by the boys.

"Wind's shifted northwest," he remarked. "Going to be cooler tomorrow an' settled weather, I reckon."

Andy, fifteen and lanky, sniffed the breeze that came down across the Cape. It no longer smelled of the sea and the salt meadows. There was a scent of clover blossoms in it, and the pungence of Jersey cedar. A huge bird sailed overhead on broad wings and settled on a nest of sticks that topped a pole behind the barn.

"Did you see that, Dad?" Andy exclaimed. "Old fish hawk had a weakfish in his claws. Real big one, too. Must have weighed more'n a pound. I shouldn't wonder if they were running in the channel now."

His father turned and looked at him with a slow wink. "Maybe it's time to count the cattle," he remarked. "Jess an' Luke can help me with the hoeing, I guess. You take Shep, an' go ahead over to the island tomorrow. Stay overnight if you like. You might see if there's any fish, while you're at it."

The boy grinned delightedly. Most Cape May County farmers would have acted differently, he knew. They were church-going Baptists in Middle Township, and believed that plenty of hard work was what boys needed. Also, in that year of 1820, it took dawn-to-dark labor by all hands to make a living. But Jeremiah Corson had liked to fish and hunt in his own boyhood. If he could find a good excuse to let his youngest son get away for a day's fishing, it gave him almost as much pleasure as if he went himself.

Jesse, who was nineteen, and Luke, the seventeen-year-old second son, would probably grumble that their young brother was a spoiled brat. But neither one was as good a fisherman as Andy. And in the fall, when ducks were flying, it was the youngest boy and his father who brought home the biggest bags.

Andy sped back into the house and up to his room under the eaves. Out of the closet he dug his handlines and sinkers. There was also a little tin box of fishhooks that had come all the way from Philadelphia. He tucked the tackle inside his shirt so that the older boys wouldn't see it, and smuggled it out to a hiding place behind the oat bin in the barn.

It was still light enough, when he came out, to see barn swallows darting through the dusk. He went out around the barn and looked up at the fish hawk's nest. Both the big birds were there. The male, with his crested white head and white breast, was perched on the outer rim of the mass of sticks. The mother hawk could just be seen above the edge of the nest. She was sitting patiently on the two big spotted eggs that Andy had seen the day before.

Fish hawks, or ospreys, to give them their proper name, were welcome guests on half the farms in the county. They were quiet, hard-working birds that never molested the chickens, ducks or geese. And it was a common belief that they kept hen hawks, owls and other marauders away.

Andy's thoughts were still on tomorrow's trip to the island. It would be more fun, he decided, if he could have company. There were several boys his own age in the neighborhood, and he set off down the road at a run, his bare feet kicking up the loose sand. The Swain farm was less than half a mile southward, in the direction of Middle Town, and Ned Swain was his closest friend.

When he got there, however, he found Ned had already gone to bed and Mr. Swain told him with disapproval that there was far too much work ahead for Ned to go gallivanting off.

Heading northward again, Andy passed his own house and went on up the road to the Amos Hand place. Young Joe Hand answered his whistle from the lighted kitchen and stole out to meet him a moment later. His hands were wet and he smelled of soap.

"Washin' dishes," he whispered. "We're not as lucky as you. No girls to do 'em. What's up?"

"Dad's sending me to Seven Mile Beach tomorrow," Andy told him. "Got to count the cattle. I can stay overnight on the island, an' I bet there'll be some fish. Can you go?"

"Gee—I'd sure like to! There isn't a bit o' chance,

though. With fair weather comin', we've got to start cuttin' hay in the south meadow tomorrow."

Andy said good night and went out to the road again. There was one other lad he might ask. Joshua Ludlam. But Josh lived more than a mile away, over toward Dennis Creek, and it was already past nine o'clock. Reluctantly the boy turned homeward. He would have to enjoy the excursion by himself.

By daylight next morning he was up and out of the house, hustling to get the chores done. He milked the three cows allotted to him, carried in the milk and filled the woodbox. Then he washed, and ate a hasty breakfast. He filled a little sack with corn meal, wrapped some salt in a piece of paper, filled his pockets with doughnuts and was out of the kitchen before the others came in.

Down cellar he went to the brine barrel and cut himself a chunk of fat salt pork. He could hear his brothers washing at the sink over his head.

"Where's the sprout?" asked Luke, good-naturedly. "Never knew him to be late for vittles."

"Oh, he's eaten already," Becky's voice answered. "He's gone off somewhere. Boys are queer creatures."

Andy grinned at the idea of his thirteen-year-old sister trying to sound grown-up. He wrapped all his provisions in an old bag and went out to the barn, where he gathered up his fishing tackle and an ancient iron frying pan. Old Shep, the collie, wagged his tail with pleasure when the boy motioned him to follow, and together they hurried across the road. At least, Andy thought, he would have the dog to talk to if he got lonesome.

The sun had risen out of the sea and made a bright path across the flooded marsh, as they went down the sandy trail between gnarled old cedar trees. It was a good half mile to the landing at the head of Great Sound.

The boat was there, pulled up and turned over at the edge of the marsh. It was a heavy, flat-bottomed skiff with oars and a small leg-o-mutton sail. There was no centerboard, but a three-inch keel made the craft sailable where no tacking was involved.

Andy had to put forth all his strength to tip the skiff right side up. Luckily the tide was high and he had to drag it only a few feet to get it into the water. He shipped the oars, stowed his duffel in the bow and jumped aboard. Shep was already sitting on his haunches in the stern, grinning from ear to ear. The old collie had been on such trips before.

With a westerly breeze coming off the land, Andy stepped the mast and let out the sheet. He could run before the wind for nearly two miles out across the Sound. Steering with an oar in the stern chock, the boy squinted into the sun ahead. Beyond the broad stretch of water loomed the wooded dunes of Seven Mile Beach—Leaming's Island, as it was more commonly called. It was still too far away to see any cattle moving, but he knew they were there. For a generation the Corsons and Leamings had ferried young stock out to pasture on this lonely bit of coast. There was good grass in the savannas behind the high dunes, and little fresh-water ponds gave the cattle a chance to drink. Living there far from any human care they were nearly as wild as deer.

For the most part the cows and their calves led a peaceful enough existence. When captured and brought to the mainland they were usually fat and well fed. There had been times, though, when they were in constant danger.

Andy had heard tales of Revolutionary days, and again of the War of 1812, when the crews of enemy ships made a regular practice of slaughtering wild cattle on the sea islands whenever they needed fresh meat. He had been only nine when the last war ended, but he still remembered the anger of neighboring farmers whose herds had been raided by British seamen.

At low tide he would have taken the channel to the south of Gull Island. But now there was plenty of water over the shoals and he headed straight across for the northerly passage—Gull Island Thorofare. From the flooded marsh where they nested, hundreds of black-capped laughing gulls rose circling and screaming.

As soon as he passed the upper point of the island Andy had to lower the sail and start rowing, for the channel made a southward bend. But it swung to the east again after a few minutes and led straight toward his destination. The boy guided the skiff into a little cove and beached it there.

Most of the day was still ahead of him. After all he had been sent to do a job and it seemed a good idea to get it out of the way first and let the fishing wait till later. He left his provisions under a tarpaulin in the boat and followed Shep, who was bounding eagerly off along the shore.

The inner side of the big island was low and marshy. In a few minutes, however, they came to a faintly marked cattle trail, leading eastward toward higher ground. The marsh grass soon gave way to bushes and scrub cedars, and a few more steps brought them into the cool shade of real woods. There were white oaks, hollies, sassafras and gum trees growing thick around a kind of glade where the meadow grass was tall and lush.

The cattle track led straight to a little pool, fringed with reeds. At Andy's approach a big blue heron straightened up from his frog-hunting and rose into the air with a flapping of mighty wings. The boy knelt by the pool and tasted the water. It was fresh and pure, with no brackish flavor. He joined Shep in a good drink and moved on toward the dunes. Beyond them he could hear the booming of surf on the beach and he hastened his steps, eager for a glimpse of the sea.

All along the outer rim of the island were hills of blown sand, forty feet high in many places. Andy toiled upward over a saddle in the dune, where twisted old cedars leaned away from the wind. At the top he paused a moment. There, spread before him, was the whole Atlantic Ocean. It glittered bright in the sunlight, stretching away league after league to the horizon. And right at his feet the waves rolled in, the white spray from their crests flying back like horses' manes.

It was a sight no boy could resist. Quickly Andy stripped off his shirt and pantaloons, dropped them in a heap under a juniper bush, and raced Shep down the slope to the beach. Together they splashed out through the shallow water and plunged headfirst into the breakers.

For twenty minutes they played in the cold, bracing surf. At last Andy picked a big wave just before it broke, launched his body on the crest and rode it all the way in at race-horse speed. Shep emerged right at his heels. The collie dashed along the beach, shaking salt water out of his shaggy coat, and the boy ran with him till the sun dried his skin. It was an exhilarating feeling to be all alone on that wild and beautiful shore, with only the dog and the screaming gulls for company.

But he remembered he still had work to do. Putting on his clothes again, he started northward up the beach. Every few minutes he went to the top of the dunes to reconnoiter. There were plenty of signs of cattle everywhere, but none appeared fresh. Once or twice Shep ran off into the woods as if he expected to find part of the herd. Andy waited to hear him bark, but each time the old dog returned without announcing any discovery.

They continued to work their way northward for an hour. By that time the boy was hungry and he sat down on a driftwood log to share some of his doughnuts with the collie. While he ate, Andy was looking about him. The beach, above the tide line, was littered with drift. There were old logs and planks and whitened ship's timbers half buried in the sand. He was watching a fiddler crab darting in and out of its hole when his eye fell on a bit of darker wood a few yards away. Moving nearer to look at it, he found the corner of a small box protruding from the sand.

It was solid, heavy wood—mahogany, he thought—and when he lifted it something rattled inside. The box was only eight or nine inches long and half as deep, but it was firmly closed by a salt-crusted brass lock.

Andy got out his jackknife and worked at the lock for several minutes with the big blade. It was no use. He looked around for a big stone to smash the box open but decided against it. Worn and weathered as it was, he thought it was too handsome a piece to destroy. So he tucked it under his arm and set off up the beach once more.

He was now perhaps two miles from the upper end of the island. The shoreline curved outward a short distance ahead, and the wooded dunes cut off any view of Townsend's Inlet, the tidal channel that formed the northern boundary of Seven Mile Beach. But just at that moment a bit of white appeared above the trees. It was moving seaward. A few seconds later he knew it was the upper canvas of a topsail schooner, heading out of the inlet.

Fishing boats and trading craft were a common enough sight along the South Jersey coast, but they usually stayed well out. There was no settlement and no harbor at Townsend's Inlet, and shoals and tide rips at the entrance made it a dangerous passage for vessels of deep draft.

Some skipper who did not know the shore must have put in for wood or water, Andy thought. As he watched, he expected momentarily to see the schooner run aground on the treacherous sand bars. But by some miracle of luck or seamanship she sped along under full sail and was soon making for the open sea. He knew most of the ships that sailed from Cape Island, Tuckahoe and the other county ports, and this was none of them. There was a rakish tilt to her masts and an odd cut to her canvas. And she had speed—plenty of it. He climbed the dunes, watching the strange schooner till she was hull-down on the southeast horizon.

CHAPTER II

SHEP HAD MOVED off into the woods west of the dunes, and Andy followed him. At any moment now he thought he would find the cattle, and he went carefully, picking up a good-sized stick to use in case one of the wild cows charged him. After a while he caught up with the collie and they beat northward through the brush till they were within sight of Townsend's Inlet. Somehow they had missed the herd, or else the cows had moved to the southern end of the island, below the place where Andy had landed.

Turning back, the boy skirted the edge of the

marshes, west of the woods. That was the only way to be sure he had not passed the cattle while moving up the beach. Shep trotted in and out of the undergrowth, searching the savannas. But not once did he bark to show he had found anything.

By the time they got back to the boat it was well past noon. The tide was out now, and it was hardly the best time for fishing. Still, Andy figured he knew now where the cattle would be, and he might as well put off the counting until later.

He had to drag the skiff several yards to reach the water. When he was ready to push off he thrust his stick into the mud and in a few seconds had dug up several good-sized clams. Then he rowed out into the channel and dropped anchor off a grassy point.

As the boat swung southward with the outgoing tide, Andy laid out his tackle. With his knife he opened one of the clams and baited a hook. The sinker went overboard with a plop. For ten or fifteen minutes he sat patiently, jiggling the bait from time to time. Finally he felt a nibble, then a sharp tug. Hauling in the line he got the hook nearly to the surface when he saw to his disgust that a large crab was chewing at the bait. He shook it off, rowed out into deeper water and anchored once more.

This time his luck was better. He caught a small

flounder and two porgies in quick succession. After that he waited more than an hour till the tide turned without getting another bite. That was normal. He knew better than to expect good fishing at slack tide. But when the current began to flow northward again he was ready with a freshly baited line. Before sunset he had pulled in four more fish, none of them very large but all good pan-size.

Just as he was starting to row back to shore, he looked northeastward across the water and saw a gray sail moving above the marshy flats. It was at least five miles away and barely visible. But he thought he recognized the rig. There was only one craft of that type in the neighborhood—Beasley Gillen's bay garvey. Gillen had a farm close to the shore of Stites Sound and used the clumsy, flat-bottomed scow to haul marsh hay from the meadows. Why he should be sailing seaward at that hour in the evening puzzled Andy, but he gave it only a moment's thought. After all, Gillen wasn't much of a farmer, and he was regarded by the neighbors as surly and unfriendly. What he chose to do with his time was none of the boy's business. He turned his attention back to handling the oars.

Andy beached the boat and set the anchor well above high water mark, so that it wouldn't drift away when the tide rose. Then, with the fish and his duffel, he went up the path to the little glade he had found earlier in the day. It would make a fine camping place, handy to the fresh-water pool and with plenty of firewood close by.

He picked a sandy spot to build his fire and brought several armfuls of dry sticks. Withered grass served for tinder. In a few moments he had the blaze started and proceeded to clean the fish. Two of them made a supper for Shep. The others, rolled in corn meal, were put into the skillet to fry with a slice of fat pork. Before darkness came, Andy had eaten his fill.

He had no blankets, but the summer night was warm. He pulled enough dry grass to make a soft bed, threw some green leaves on the fire for a smudge, and lay down with Shep close beside him. In spite of the smoke a few mosquitoes buzzed about, but he hardly noticed them. Like most Jerseymen he had a tough hide and a bite or two never bothered him.

He slept soundly for several hours. It must have been nearly dawn when the collie stirred suddenly and woke him. Shep barked once or twice, then stood alert, listening. Andy sat up.

"What is it, boy?" he whispered. Then he, too, heard the sound—a distant bellowing of cattle. To his surprise, the noise seemed to come from the northern part of the island, where he had already searched. He had been sure he would find the herd down by Hereford Inlet. Now it appeared they must have moved north again in the night, or in the afternoon while he was fishing.

The bellowing stopped after a minute or two and the boy lay down again and slept. When daylight roused him, he saw Shep prowling restlessly about the little meadow. The dog came bounding toward him, whined once or twice and started northward, looking back over his shoulder.

Andy laughed. "Sure—we'll go an' round up the cows," he told the collie. "But there's no rush. We're going to eat breakfast first."

He built a fresh fire and mixed corn meal with salt and water to make journey-cakes. Fried in the skillet they tasted better than they looked. Even Shep, eager as he was to be off, gulped down one of the crisp, yellow cakes and licked his lips.

"All right," the boy told him, "let's go!"

The dog gave every indication that this time he knew where he was headed. He went at a steady trot, and Andy had to hurry to keep him in sight. Soon they picked up fresh cattle signs. The tracks in the mud pointed north.

For two or three miles the trail led through the woods in the middle of the island. Then it swung to the right, crossing a saddle in the dunes. The loose sand above the beach seemed to have been tossed about by milling hoofs, though there were no clear tracks. Suddenly Shep raced ahead. Looking up the beach, Andy saw two big birds circling low over the sand. For a moment he thought they were fish hawks. Then he noticed their dark plumage and the five feathers, like spread fingers, at the tip of each broad wing. They were turkey buzzards.

Even the dog's approach failed to scare the huge birds away. One of them had lighted awkwardly on the ground and was tearing at something that lay there in the sand. It was only when Andy came close that the scavengers flapped off to perch in a dead tree on the dune. He had a sick feeling as he looked down at the thing they had been eating. It was a yearling heifer, her brown hide torn and bloody, and her hind quarters completely cut away. In spite of the more recent ravages of the buzzards there was no question about the knife marks on her flanks, or the dried patch of blood under the gaping slash in her throat. That was the work of men.

Andy looked more closely at the poor beast's head. She bore the Corson earmark—a deep swallowtail notch in the tip of the left ear that served to distinguish their cattle from those belonging to the other farmers. He hesitated a moment, then cut off the ear with his knife. When he told his father about this, he knew he should have some evidence.

After that he looked about for other clues to what

had happened. A hundred yards away, in a hollow at the foot of the dune, he came on the cold, dead ashes of a fire. It must have been a big one, for the burnt sticks covered an area of eight or ten feet. Drift logs had been pulled up in a semicircle around it, and there were many tracks in the sand—not cattle tracks this time but the marks of men's feet. Blurred as they were he could make out the prints of bare feet and feet in sea boots. And they were of different sizes. At least a dozen men must have been there.

Half buried in the sand were gnawed beef bones with a few shreds of meat still clinging to them. Andy tried to figure how long ago the feast had taken place. His first thought was of Beasley Gillen's boat, sailing toward the island at twilight. But if the farmer was guilty of cattle-killing he would hardly have barbecued the meat on the beach. It seemed more likely that he would have taken it home. Also the size of the fire and the many footprints suggested a large party of men.

Then, in a flash, Andy remembered the schooner he had seen the previous day. That was the answer, he was sure. The heifer must have been slaughtered, not last night, but the night before. In his hunt for the cattle he remembered he had left the beach some distance south and cut inland, searching the woods. Otherwise he would have discovered the carcass a day earlier.

Shep had kept up a steady, low growling ever since they had come on the dead heifer. He sensed that something was very wrong. Now Andy urged him to follow the men's tracks, but after casting about a little he trotted down the beach toward the water. There he stood looking back at his young master.

"I've got it," the boy told him. "You mean they came in a boat an' left the same way."

He had reached the same conclusion himself, for it was obvious that no footprints led over the dune. He called the dog and they started up the sand and into the woods.

"Go find the cows, Shep," he said. "We've got to see how many others are gone."

When the cattle had been put on the island in the early spring, there had been forty-three head. Nineteen belonged to his father and the rest were the property of the Leamings and Swains. The chances were that several calves had been born since then, and he had expected to find close to fifty in all.

The collie picked up the trail without difficulty and led the way northward at a good pace. They had gone less than half a mile when they came to a narrow path, twisting between the trunks of the trees. It was a dark and eerie place. Andy thought twice before he followed the dog into it, but after cutting himself a club from an oak sapling he plunged after him. Then he heard Shep bark.

Within twenty paces the thick growth ended suddenly and Andy found himself at the edge of a swampy savanna. On the farther side of it, huddled together as if for protection, stood the cattle. From the way they stared and tossed their heads he could see that they were nervous and "spooky." He called Shep back and stood quietly, waiting for them to get used to the look and scent of their visitors.

After a while he began calling softly—"So, boss, here, boss—co-boss." Some of the older cows seemed to remember the words and the tone. One old brindle left the herd and took a few hesitant steps toward him. The tension relaxed a little, but they still kept their eyes on the boy and the dog. Not one of them dropped its head to graze.

Slowly Andy walked toward them, talking in the same low, soothing voice. When he had advanced about twenty yards he was near enough to distinguish some of the earmarks. There were eight young calves, still unbranded, staying close to their mothers. As nearly as he could count, the number of cows and yearling heifers was either forty-one or forty-two. The cattle were packed so tightly together that he could not be certain.

From where he stood he could spot seven or eight

cows with the swallowtail cut in the left ear. The Swain earmarks were more complicated. The tip of each ear was slit, and a semicircle, known as a "half-penny," was cut out of the lower side of the right ear. Jonathan Leaming's cattle had both ears cropped off square at the tips.

Making an accurate count of the different brands would be impossible, Andy saw, unless he could get the cows to move out of their huddle. He had been holding Shep by the ruff. Now he released his grip.

"Go easy, boy," he told the dog. "They're still jumpy."

The old collie seemed to understand. He went forward cautiously, not heading directly toward the herd but quartering across the meadow. The cattle watched him with rolling eyes, shifting their feet uneasily. Then, without warning, the old brindle lowered her horns and charged at the dog.

Shep jumped aside and whirled to nip at her heels as she went by. But now the whole herd was in commotion. With a clashing of horns the cattle broke ranks and stampeded, heading straight toward Andy.

The boy knew better than to try to stop that wild rush. He turned and sprinted back to the woods with the nearest cow only seconds behind him. He dropped his stick, jumped as high as he could and caught hold of the overhanging branch of a gum tree. As he hauled himself up, the cattle went past below him, smashing through the thickets without slackening pace. Within a minute the savanna was empty and the sound of the frightened herd grew fainter as they galloped away down the island.

Shep came limping across the meadow and looked up at his master in the tree. His expression said as plainly as words, "I'll chase 'em if you say so, but you know it's no use."

Shaken as he was by his narrow escape, Andy had to laugh. "You stay here with me, boy," he told the dog. "Our job is to get out of here with whole skins if we can."

He let himself down and examined the collie's fore-paw. It had been stepped on in the stampede, but no bones seemed to be broken. Going on three legs he would be able to travel fairly well.

They went westward toward the edge of the marsh beyond the woods. Andy was sure the cattle would keep to the cover of the trees and he wanted to steer clear of any more encounters with them. After an hour's steady walking the boy and the dog reached the place where the boat was pulled up. It had shifted with the tide but the anchor had held firm.

Andy put the skillet aboard, pushed the skiff down to the water and followed Shep over the gunwale. It was when he was picking up the oars that he saw the little mahogany chest under the thwart where he had placed it the night before. Other events had made him completely forget it until that moment. Now his curiosity returned. As soon as he got home he would try once more to open it. Perhaps the box had some connection with the mysterious schooner and its cattle-killing crew.

The tide was on the ebb and against him now. But the wind had swung into the southeast. He spread the little sail and the skiff moved slowly up the channel toward Great Sound.

CHAPTER III

ANDY WAS HUNGRY when he got home. The noon hour was past and his father and brothers had eaten and gone back to their hoeing, but Mrs. Corson soon had a lunch for him on the kitchen table. While he drank a second mug of milk and munched a fourth doughnut he told her about the slaughtered cow.

"It was one of our heifers," he said. "I brought the ear home. Here it is." And he fished the blood-stained thing from his pocket, much to his mother's distress.

"Goodness!" she exclaimed. "What's the world coming to? We've pastured cattle for years on that island an' they've been safe ever since the war. You'd better go out right now an' tell your father."

Andy hid the little mahogany box in the barn and headed for the potato field. Jeremiah Corson paused in the middle of a row and mopped his tanned face. It was a hot afternoon.

"How'd you find 'em, son?" he asked.

"They were so spooky, I never did get a full count," the boy replied. "But I think there's only one missing, an' eight new calves. I found the dead heifer. Somebody killed her on the beach night before last. Most o' the meat was gone, an' they'd had a big fire an' cooked it."

Again he pulled out the ear and handed it to his father.

The elder Corson frowned. "That's our mark, right enough," he said. "Brown heifer with a white patch on her flank. Old Betsy's calf. I remember making this cut, last time we branded. Any way to tell who did it?"

By this time the other boys had come up and were examining the ear with interest.

"First off," Andy said, "I thought it was Beasley Gillen. He was coming out o' Stites Sound in his garvey last night around dusk."

"That's right," Luke put in. "I was over there to see Prue. The old man shoved off on the evening tide. Nobody with him but Jim, his colored man."

"Well," Andy continued, "it couldn't have been Gillen, because the heifer'd been dead longer'n that when I found her this morning. Besides, there were a lot o' tracks—I'd say a dozen men—an' they'd all sat around a big fire while they cooked the meat. I figure it was night before last because yesterday I sighted a schooner coming out o' Townsend's Inlet."

"Fishermen, I reckon," said Jesse. "Some o' those low-down cusses from up the coast."

Andy shook his head. "This didn't look like any Jersey-built ship," he told them. "She was fast, with queer-cut topsails an' quite a rake to her masts. She sure knew her way 'round, though. Went right out through the shoals an' never scraped her keel."

"Guess I'll have to go over there myself an' look things over," Jeremiah Corson grunted. "When's the next high tide?"

"Not till about seven tonight," Andy told him. "Can I go, Dad?"

"Yes—you an' Jess. We'll need you to show us where you found the dead cow. Get to work now, all of you. We'll have to hustle to get the chores done an' be out there before dark."

They finished the milking by six-thirty and hurried through their supper. When they set off for the landing, Jess was carrying a shovel and his father had his old flintlock fowling-piece, loaded with buckshot.

The tide was at flood and they had neither wind nor current to help them at first. But Jess took the oars and his powerful strokes sent the skiff along at a good pace. He was a big youngster, six-feet-two and broad-shouldered, strong as a bull.

There was still some daylight left when they beached the boat in the cove on the island.

"How far is it?" Jeremiah Corson asked.

"About three miles in all," said Andy. "We'll make better time if we cut across an' go up the beach."

Shep had been left at home on this trip, but the boy would have known the way blindfolded. He started at a trot, with his father and brother striding close behind. Once, in the cedar growth, they stopped to examine fresh cattle tracks. Jess called "Co-boss!" a few times but there was no answer from the cows.

"If they're as scary as Andy says, we won't see 'em," said the farmer. "They'll be holed up in the thickets somewhere."

The sun was down when they got to the beach. On the hard sand they were able to make better time and after twenty minutes of fast walking, Andy pointed ahead.

"There she is," he said. "Just above the tide line."

The buzzards and crabs had been at work on the carcass since morning. Most of the bones were stripped bare and the eyes and tongue had been torn out. Still,

Jeremiah Corson could recognize what was left of his heifer.

"Pretty nasty sight," he growled. "Well, Jess, dig a hole an' get her buried. Andy, come show me where that fire was."

He studied the charred sticks and ashes carefully, then examined the footprints in the sand.

"You're right," he said finally. "Quite a party o' men were here. What's that you got? Find something?"

The boy had stepped on a sharp object buried in the sand close to one of the driftwood logs. At first he thought it was a broken clamshell, but when he scraped the sand away he discovered a big, broad-bladed knife with a carved bone handle.

His father looked at it. "Seaman's dirk," he said. "That carving looks foreign, though. Spanish or Portuguese, I reckon. A lot o' these coasting traders sign on sailors in the Spanish Islands."

Jesse had finished his grave-digging and joined them. "That's right," he said. "I remember Zeb Hand found a knife like that year before last when the schooner was wrecked down the beach here, in a big winter storm."

His father nodded. "She was out o' Havana, loaded with rum an' silk an' cigars," he replied. "I always suspected she was a smuggler, but there was no way to tell. All hands lost."

"I remember there was a wreck, all right," said Andy. "But where is it now?"

"Maybe a mile down-shore," his brother told him. "We passed the place. Sometimes at real low tide you can see her ribs above water."

"Come on, boys," said Jeremiah Corson. "It'll be plumb dark before we get through the woods if we don't move smart."

They stumbled out of the cedar growth an hour later, feeling their way the last part of the journey. Once the boat was launched and Jess started rowing, there was light enough on the water for Andy to steer by. He kept to the channel as they bucked an ebbing tide all the way up the Sound.

"Dad," he said, "do you s'pose that schooner I saw was a smuggler?"

His father shook his head. "Don't know what smugglers would be doing in Townsend's Inlet," he replied. "There's no way for 'em to get to the mainland. They'd be more likely to head for Absecon or some other place up the coast. Besides, we've all been decent, law-abiding folks 'round here for generations. It takes rogues on land as well as on the sea to smuggle goods ashore."

"Well," Andy persisted, "the ship looked queer to me. Whatever they were up to, they probably anchored inside the inlet because they knew there were cattle here an' they could steal some fresh meat."

He was silent the rest of the way home, but his thoughts were on the wreck of two winters before. The place where he had found the mahogany chest must have been very close to it. And the condition of the box suggested that it had lain for many months in the sand. He was more eager than ever to try to open it.

It was well past their usual bedtime when the Corsons reached the farm, and Andy was so tired that he could hardly keep his eyes open while he undressed. He slept like a log. At sun-up Luke hauled him out of bed or he would probably have lain there till noon.

A light rain had started to fall in the night. That meant there would be no field work, and as soon as the chores were done and breakfast eaten, Andy stole out to the barn and got the box from its hiding place. With a chisel out of the tool cabinet he worked on the lock until he had loosened the brass screws that held it. Carefully he pried up the lid and looked inside.

At first all he saw was gray sand and salt that had sifted in. Then, as he picked up the box, the edge of a silver disc appeared. He removed it and saw that it was a Spanish dollar—a coin such as trading vessels to the West Indies sometimes brought into the coastal ports.

He tipped the little chest over, hoping to find more,

but all that fell out was more sand and a small piece of wood. Disappointed, he was about to toss away the wooden sliver when he felt something like carving on its surface. He brushed off the sand and discovered there were letters cut into it with a knife. As nearly as he could make out the crude carving, it read:

SIGNEL T. INLET
S. 700 to †
WT. 1 TYDE

That was all. The queer-shaped symbol above and to the right of the cross looked a little like a flying bird. Andy was still puzzling over the inscription when he heard footsteps and hastily returned the bit of wood to the box. He stooped to hide his find behind the grain bin. Before he could straighten up, his younger sister Becky came into the barn.

"I've been looking all over for you," she said. "Mother wants you to run an errand down to the store. Why, Andy Corson—what were you putting in there?"

He had learned long ago it was hopeless to try to keep secrets from Becky. Quick as a flash she darted to the grain bin and pulled out the little chest. Andy snatched it from her.

"You promise you won't tell a living soul?" he asked with a scowl.

"Cross my heart," she replied solemnly.

"All right," he said, lowering his voice. "I found it on the beach. It was mostly covered up by sand an' it must have been there a long time. I think it came from that schooner that got wrecked a couple o' winters back."

"What's in it?" she whispered. "I heard something rattle."

He lifted the cover and showed her the contents.

"That's silver, isn't it?" she exclaimed, fingering the foreign coin. "But what's that writing mean on the piece of wood?"

"I haven't figured it out yet. Something about a signal, and waiting one tide. I thought 'T. Inlet' might mean Townsend's Inlet, but what that second line's about I couldn't tell you."

Becky studied the inscription and her eyes began sparkling with excitement. "Why, look!" she said. "That's a bird flying—and the cross thing must be a tree!"

Andy nodded thoughtfully. "A tree," he murmured. "A tree where a bird roosts. Maybe a fish hawk's nest? But I still don't see why a ship from Cuba would be keeping something like this so carefully—locked up in a special box."

He replaced the little chest in the secret place behind the grain bin. "We'll both keep figuring on it," he told his sister. "Perhaps one of us'll think of the answer."

They went back to the house together and found Mrs. Corson in a flurry of baking.

"I declare," she said, rolling piecrust energetically, "any time you're needed, Andy, you have the worst habit of disappearing. Saddle up now an' go to the village for me. I want five pounds o' sugar. Here's the money. With the high tariff the government's put on the stuff, you'd think it was gold. It'll take pretty near a dollar to buy that much. Bring back the change, an' be sure you keep the sugar dry."

Andy wrapped himself in an oilskin slicker, saddled the black colt that he had raised with his own hands, and set off for Middle Town. Two miles down the road, it was little more than a cluster of a dozen houses, a general store, a tavern and two churches. But the fact that it was the county seat gave the place some importance. Most of its activities centered around the courthouse and the little wooden jail.

The rain was still falling steadily when Andy tied Starlight to the hitching rail and went into the store. It was dark inside and smelled of stale crackers, pickle brine, molasses and fish. Two old chairs and a three-legged stool in the middle of the cluttered floor were occupied at the moment by Enoch Hughes, the storekeeper, and a couple of loafers who made the place their headquarters. They glanced at Andy, saw he was only a boy and went on with their conversation.

"Sure, I reco'nized her," said Dode Gowdy. "I was out clammin', over on the south marsh. There ain't many schooners with that cut o' sail."

The third man was a small, rat-faced fellow with a wooden leg. He was supposed to have had his leg shot off in a naval engagement during the late war, but there were those who said he had lost it trying to break out of jail. The only name he went by around the village was "Stumpy."

He chuckled at Gowdy's words and stole a glance in Andy's direction. "Looks like there might be some hayin' done," he mumbled, and the others laughed as if he had cracked a joke.

Enoch Hughes stood up and stretched. "What can I do for you, sonny?" he inquired.

Andy stated his errand and saw the sugar weighed out. "How much?" he asked.

"Well," said the storekeeper, "the duty's pretty high, ye know. Sugar's gone up two cents this week. Nineteen a pound now. That's ninety-five cents."

Andy whistled as he took his five cents change.

"Yep," said Hughes sympathetically. "I know it's too high a price. That's what makes smugglin' popular." He turned his face away and Andy thought he must have winked at his cronies, for they were grinning as the boy left the store.

He buttoned his slicker tightly over the package to keep it from getting wet, untied Starlight's reins and mounted. A smoldering resentment filled him as he galloped the young horse homeward. He tried to recall the exact words of Stumpy's gibe. It went something like "Guess there'll be some hayin' done," and he had no doubt it was aimed at himself. So they thought he was a hayseed and joked about it—a bunch of no-good clam-diggers and town drunks!

It wasn't until the boy was inside the barn and wiping down his horse that he cooled off. It occurred to him then for the first time that the trio in the store might have been talking about something quite different—something they didn't want him to understand. And he had a half-formed suspicion that the strange schooner was a part of it.

CHAPTER IV

FRIDAY WAS AN IMPORTANT DAY at the farm. That was when the weekly edition of the Philadelphia paper usually arrived. Once in a while a letter came for the Corsons in the old mail stage that lumbered overland and down the Cape, taking three or four days on the way. During the summer, however, most mail was carried by the steamboat. City people had begun to discover the pleasures of ocean bathing, and three times a week a small, puffing side-wheeler brought forty or fifty ladies and gentlemen down the Delaware, reaching Cape May the same day it left Philadelphia.

Andy had seen the bathers once, when his father had business at Cape Island. The men looked pretty funny to him, in their long bathing drawers and striped jerseys. No doubt the women looked queerer still, but it was considered improper for any males to watch them when they went down to the water, so the boy remained in ignorance.

On this particular Friday it was noon when the newspaper came. The weather had cleared after the rain and all three boys had been helping their father in the field. But when dinner was over, Jeremiah Corson sat down to read them the news of the outside world.

"Hmm," he said, adjusting his spectacles. "Seems as if there's been such a hullabaloo raised about high tariffs, the Congress might decide to do something. Some o' the speeches sound real hot under the collar. One feller called it the 'Tariff of Abominations.' Pretty good name, eh?"

He chuckled to himself and peered up and down the columns for other bits of news.

"Quite a few advertisements for runaway slaves," he commented. "Poor cusses—I hope they don't catch 'em. Horses for sale—a hundred an' fifty dollars for a matched pair o' four-year-old drafters. Tch, tch—what a price! Here's an item about our own county. It says 'Revenue Cutter *Valiant,* ten guns, ordered to Cape May.' Seems like they've got the smugglers pretty well stopped in the Bay, but goods are still getting to Philadelphia some other way. I wonder—Egg Harbor, maybe, or Barnegat? Anyhow, the *Valiant's* going to patrol off the Cape."

"That's right," said Jesse. "I heard she was anchored at the mouth o' Dennis Creek. Some of her crew came ashore last night, Mordecai Williams told me."

Shortly after, they went back to hoeing potatoes. It was a hot afternoon with little breeze stirring. About three o'clock Andy's father sent him back to the house to fetch a jug of water from the well. He was just pulling up the bucket when a big, bony man on an equally bony horse rode into the yard.

There was something so awkward about the stranger that Andy wanted to laugh. His stirrups were too short and his knees stuck out at an uncomfortable angle. He hauled hard on the reins and brought the nag to a stop just short of the well curb. Gingerly, as if unused to saddles, he eased himself to the ground.

"Good day, lad," the man remarked, politely enough. "Could I get some water for my horse? I could stand a drop or two myself."

"Sure," said Andy. He poured from the bucket into a half coconut shell that sat on the curb. "Drink this, an' I'll fill the horse trough."

The stranger smacked his lips as he finished. "Hot day for riding," he said. "Whose farm is this?"

"Belongs to my father, Jeremiah Corson."

"I see you're pretty close to the marsh here. Ever get out to those islands along the beach?"

"Sure—all the time," Andy replied. "We've got a boat here at the head o' the Sound. Some of our cattle are pastured over on Seven Mile Beach."

The man's gray eyes looked at the boy sharply, but his long, weather-browned face did not change expression.

"Nice set o' buildings you've got," he said. "Mind if I look around?"

Without waiting for an answer he set off at a long, rolling stride, and Andy kept pace with him. He didn't wholly trust this cool fellow.

At the rear of the barn the stranger paused suddenly, looking up at the pole that supported the fish hawks' nest.

"What do you call that?" he asked.

"That's where our fish hawks live," the boy replied tartly. "We've had 'em for 'most five years. That's the mother one sitting on her eggs."

The man nodded but his eyes turned from the nest

to Andy. There was a cold glint in them and his mouth was set in a hard line.

"I'll look a bit more," he announced abruptly and went into the barn, opening doors, peering into grain bins and climbing the ladder to scan the empty hayloft.

Andy's anger was rising. "I don't know what you're after," he blurted at last, "but you'd better wait till my dad gets here before you look any farther."

The tall man looked at him and laughed suddenly. "All right, sonny," he said. "What I was looking for doesn't seem to be here anyway, so I'll up anchor."

He returned to the well, clambered aboard his horse and waved a long arm in farewell as they ambled off up the road.

Andy watched the stranger out of sight. Then he grabbed up the jug of water and hurried back to the field.

"What kept you so long?" Luke asked testily. "Didn't you know we were thirsty?"

Andy waited for his father to come up before he explained the delay. "I'd say the man was more used to ships than horses," he concluded. "He rode as if it hurt him, an' jerked at the reins like a sailor hauling the yards. The queer thing, though, was that he didn't get really snoopy till after he'd seen the fish hawks' nest. That started him an' he didn't quit till he'd gone over the barn, top to bottom."

"Hmm," said Jeremiah Corson, glowering. "Wish I'd been there. He wouldn't ha' got far. Unless he was a sheriff's officer he had no business to search another man's property, an' even then he'd need a warrant. Which way'd he go?"

"Up the road," Andy replied, "toward the Hand place."

His father said no more about it until the hoeing was done, but that evening after supper he saddled a horse and rode north. He came home less than an hour later, his face still grim.

"Nobody knows who the fellow was," he told the boys. "But he went through the same performance at Hands'. Stopped at Jenkins', too, but soon as he found they didn't have any fish hawks around he just rode off. Sounds to me as if he must be crazy."

Andy wondered, after he went to bed that night. The man had acted sane enough, but there was something about fish hawks' nests that made him become suddenly dangerous. In the morning he got hold of Becky and they went off together where they could talk privately. She wanted to know all about the appearance of the strange visitor, and he told her.

"You don't suppose," he said, "that this fish hawk business has anything to do with the carving on that piece o' wood I found, do you? Remember—you thought it was a tree an' a bird?"

Becky's eyes grew big with excitement. "Why, of course!" she exclaimed. "He's a pirate or a smuggler, you can be sure! Did he look Spanish?"

Andy laughed. "About as much as you do," he said. "No, Beck, you've got to come up with a better idea than that. Still, I keep thinking there might be some connection——"

"Say!" the girl interrupted. "He didn't *find* the little box, did he?"

"No. I was afraid he would for a minute, but he must have been looking for something bigger an' bulkier. I could tell that from the places he hunted."

The mystery wasn't solved that day or the next. The Sabbath was strictly observed by the farm families along the Cape road. No unnecessary work was done, and everybody who was able went to church. As soon as breakfast was over and the dishes washed, the whole Corson family put on Sunday clothes and got into the best wagon, sitting on boards laid across its sides.

The farm horses moved at a sedate walk, so that the jouncing over the rough road wouldn't be too hard on the ladies. Clouds of dust ahead of them and behind them showed where neighbors were making the same journey. When they reached the Baptist Meeting House in Middle Town, a dozen teams were already tied under the trees. By ten o'clock every wooden bench in the church was filled with men, women and children, all in their Sunday best.

The service was a long one. They had a devout and earnest preacher, who felt that a sermon should be well drawn out to have any real effect on the congregation. Andy stood the first part of it fairly well, but toward the end of the second hour he began to grow restless. It seemed as if his bones would wear holes right through his trousers into the hard oak of the bench. When the closing hymn was finally announced he joined the singing with grateful fervor.

There was a scraping of boots and a rustle of starched dresses as the gathering broke up. Friendly greetings were exchanged among families who saw each other only once a week. Outside, under the trees, the men went off by themselves to talk crops and politics while the housewives discussed cooking and sewing and the latest neighborhood gossip.

The older boys made eyes at the girls, and the younger ones swapped knives and climbed fences. Andy saw Luke, off in a corner of the Meeting House yard, talking to Prudence Mayhew. Prudence was the "bound girl" who worked for the Gillens. Orphaned when she was a small child, she had been indentured as a servant. Now, at sixteen, her bond had two more years to run before she would be free. She was a thin little thing with blond hair and a gentle look in her big, dark eyes.

Andy wondered how she stood the constant labor at the Gillen place. He thought it was partly pity for her hard existence that made Luke so devoted to the girl. Certainly Beasley Gillen showed her no affection, and his wife was not the motherly type. Mrs. Gillen was talking to the storekeeper's wife now. She was a big, blowzy woman with hair that was always escaping from the knot at the back of her head and falling in strings around her red face. But her dress of brown bombazine had an expensive look and she wore gold rings on both her hands.

Ned Swain, Joe Hand and Josh Ludlam joined him and asked about his trip to the island. Word of the cattle-killing had spread. He told them the gory details of finding the dead heifer and described the fish he had caught. It was a temptation to mention the little mahogany chest, but that was a secret only he and his sister knew.

Joe Hand brought up the subject of the tall stranger on the bony nag. "That horse was from Jones's livery stable, down at the Cape," he said. "Dad recognized it. An' the fellow talked with a drawl like a Southerner. I figure he was off a coasting schooner out o' Baltimore or Charleston. Sure was a cool customer, though, the way he looked over our place."

"What did he say about fish hawks?" Andy asked.

"Nothing. Just took a look at the nest an' began searching the barn."

"Maybe he was after a runaway slave," Josh Ludlam suggested.

That was a possibility Andy hadn't considered before. If Joe was right about the Southern accent, it might explain the stranger's actions. He remembered thinking at the time that the fellow didn't sound like a Jerseyman. But why on earth should he be interested in fish hawks' nests?

Mrs. Corson began gathering her brood, anxious to get home and start cooking dinner. When they were all in the wagon the conversation turned to church matters.

"Had a good turnout today," said Jeremiah Corson. "I guess just about everybody was there but Beasley Gillen. Wonder what kept him away."

"He's off on one of his trips to Philadelphia," Luke replied. "Prue says he left Thursday morning with a load o' hay."

Jesse chuckled. "It sure beats me how he makes money out o' hauling marsh hay that far," he said. "Some o' those city folks must be awful suckers to pay a big price for that stuff."

"Gillen claims they use it to pack chinaware in barrels," Luke explained. "You'd think they could get plenty of it closer than Cape May County, but I guess ours is a special kind. Anyhow, he does get well paid. Bought a new team o' horses the last trip he made."

"That's right," the older sister, Elvira, put in. "They always seem to have money. Look at the fine dresses that woman wears. I declare she has more clothes than anyone else in Middle Township, for all she's such a frump."

Sunday afternoons were long for the young people. After a big dinner the elder Corsons took naps. The girls were allowed to do some sewing or read inspirational books. And the boys usually went for walks around the place.

Luke and Andy strolled northward along the line fence, and when they reached the corner of the farm, Luke climbed over into the road.

"You go on back," he told his younger brother. "I promised Prudence I'd come an' see her this afternoon. You don't have to tell the folks."

Chore time came that evening and Luke had still not returned. Andy and Jess did his share of the milking.

"Reckon you'd better go find him," said Jess. "Dad'll be pretty sore if he doesn't get home soon."

The younger boy set off up the road on foot. It was two or three miles to the Gillen farm, and the house and outbuildings were some distance from the highway, down near the edge of Stites Sound. Dusk had begun to fall when Andy was a mile from home. He trudged on through the twilight and after a while he saw a lone figure approaching. It was Luke, but he was coming slowly and his body was bent as if he had rheumatism.

Andy ran toward him. "What's the matter?" he called. "You get hurt or something?"

The older boy's face looked pale and drawn.

" 'Tisn't much," Luke replied, gritting his teeth. "I'll be all right, soon as I get home."

But Andy had caught a glimpse of the red splotch that stained the back of his brother's shirt.

"Wait a minute," he cried in alarm. "You're bleeding a lot an' we've got to do something about it!"

"Well—all right," Luke agreed. "This shirt's spoiled anyway. You better pull it off an' make a bandage."

Andy lost no time. With the shirt removed, he found an ugly-looking puncture in Luke's back—a small hole from which the blood was still welling slowly.

"Gosh!" he said. "What happened? Did somebody shoot you?"

Luke shook his head and winced with pain. "No," he panted. "It was a pitchfork stuck me. Tie it up now, an' don't ask any more questions."

CHAPTER V

ANDY DID THE BEST he could. He tore the shirt into strips, made a pad to go over the wound, and pulled the bandage as tightly around Luke's body as it would go.

"Now listen," he said, as they started homeward. "You know well enough you're not so clumsy you'd fall on a pitchfork. If you won't tell me what happened, I can make my own guess. Somebody jabbed you with that fork, an' I want to know why."

Luke kept silent for several steps. "All right," he blurted at last, "I'll tell you, but don't you dare say a word at home. They'd never let me go back there. I was down in the orchard with Prue when Gillen got home. He unhitched his team an' left the wagon standing in front o' the barn. After he'd gone in the house we came back through the yard. Neither one o' the Gillens like my coming around to see Prue very much. They think I take up her time when she ought to be working. Besides, it was getting late an' I knew I'd better start home.

"When we got to the wagon I happened to look in over the tailboard. There was something bright-colored caught in a crack o' the floor, an' I reached in an' pulled it out. It was a little piece o' red silk, half as big as my hand, torn in a three-cornered shape. Prue an' I were looking at it, saying how pretty it was, when Beasley came rushing out.

"He was madder'n a stung bull, we could tell from the look on his face. He hollered something an' I dropped the silk an' started to run. Then he grabbed the fork out o' the wagon an' flung it after me. Caught me in the back so hard I fell down. I got up again before he could reach me an' ran all the way to the road. Now—if you know what he was so sore about—you tell me."

Andy's face was grim with anger. "The dirty, low-down skunk!" he muttered. "He might ha' killed you. We ought to get the sheriff after him. He deserves to go to jail for that!"

"No," said Luke. "They'd just take it out on poor Prue. You an' I have got to keep this to ourselves."

They walked on in silence for a while. When Andy spoke again he had done some thinking.

"It must have been that piece o' silk," he said. "What in the world would that be doing in the bottom of a hay-cart?"

"All I can figure," Luke replied, "is that he was bringing some dress goods home to his wife. Maybe they're touchy about all the fine clothes she has."

Andy considered this idea. It didn't sound wholly plausible but for the moment he couldn't think of any better reason for the farmer's wrath.

"Well," he said at length, "we can wait an' see. If that's it, Mrs. Gillen'll be wearing red silk to church in a week or two. What worries me right now is how you're going to keep Dad an' Mother from knowing you got hurt. You'll be in poor shape to do any work."

As things turned out, it wasn't too difficult to keep the secret. The boy smuggled his brother in through the kitchen and up the back stairs. The family had already eaten supper. Andy got some cookies and milk and took them up to Luke, then had something to eat himself. After that he reported to his father and mother that Luke wasn't feeling very well.

"Maybe he ate some green apples," he said, as casually as possible. "I don't know if that was it or not, but anyhow he'll be all right now."

Mrs. Corson was all for giving the boy a dose of castor oil, but Andy succeeded in heading her off. "Luke's asleep," he said. "I figure all he needs is to be let alone."

The next morning the wound showed no signs of inflammation, and Luke claimed some of the soreness was gone. Luckily for him there was little work done that forenoon. Just after breakfast Becky came dashing in with the news that the bees were swarming.

In the big apple tree near the house they could hear the loud buzzing of thousands of excited honeybees. The swarm was beginning to form on a low-hanging branch. Jeremiah Corson went to get his gloves and bee mask and Elvira and Becky produced big milkpans and mixing spoons. With these they made a tremendous clatter, loud enough to drown out the humming of the queen bee. If the swarm should take off after her she might lead them miles away to some hollow tree in the woods.

The farmer brought a clean, empty hive and a saw from the tool rack. He waited till the swarm had formed a great, dark ball on the end of the limb, then gently sawed it off, a couple of feet from the buzzing, writhing mass. As soon as he had it off he lowered it to a board on the ground and placed the hive over the board.

"Well," said Jeremiah Corson, taking off the bee mask and mopping his brow, "that ought to give 'em the new home they want. I'll have to wait till they crawl up in the top o' the hive an' then pull the branch out. I guess that means I won't do any mowing till after dinner. You can start, though, Jess. We ought to have four or five acres done by night."

Jess whetted his scythe and set off for the upper field. The other boys would have nothing to do until the hay had cured on the ground. After that it would need turning, raking and bunching before being hauled to the barn, and all the male members of the family would have their hands full.

Andy changed the bandage on Luke's back and disposed of the torn and bloody shirt by stuffing it behind the woodpile in the shed. Sooner or later his mother would wonder why one of Luke's shirts was missing, but they would meet that problem when they came to it. Meanwhile, the wound seemed to be healing satisfactorily. A good clean scab had formed and the boy said it no longer hurt him to move. By the next morning he was able to take his place with the others in the hayfield.

Two weeks of hard, hot work followed. Load after load of sweet-smelling clover and timothy was brought to the barn and stowed in the mows. The weather favored them. Only once did a thundershower come to drench the hay in the field. And a day's hot sunshine dried it out before any damage was done.

As long as the haying went on there was no chance for Andy to go fishing or revisit the island. The little mahogany box and the queer symbols cut on the piece of wood it contained were still much in his mind, however. Occasionally he talked to Becky about the mystery. She had a lively imagination, and her ideas usually dealt with bloodthirsty pirates and buried treasure.

"If we could only figure out the directions," she said, "I bet we'd find skeletons in the sand an' a whole big chest full o' gold doubloons!"

Andy chuckled. "There hasn't been a pirate on this coast since the days o' Ned Lowe," he told her. "That was near a hundred years ago, an' since that time I reckon every foot o' the beach has been washed out, or filled in by hurricanes, or dug over by treasure hunters. Besides, we're pretty sure that little box was only on the beach a couple o' years."

Out behind the barn, the fish hawks' nest was now a scene of great activity. The eggs had hatched successfully and the two awkward, fuzzy chicks could be seen, poking their wide-open beaks above the circle of sticks.

Both parents fished from dawn to dark to supply their babies' monstrous appetites.

Andy was watching the mother bird feed them, one July evening, when his father strolled out to join him.

"Been talking to your ma," the elder Corson remarked, chewing on a straw. "She says it's your turn to go to the city an' get measured for a suit o' clothes. I guess that's fair enough, seeing's the other boys had 'em when they were your age."

Andy's eyes shone. "Gosh, Dad!" he breathed. "All the way to Philadelphia?"

The farmer nodded. "I'll have some business to 'tend to up there, so we'll go together. Horseback. I don't trust these new-fangled steamboats. We'll wait till haying's over an' the oats are in before we start. 'Round the end o' the month, I'd guess."

To Andy, who had never been out of Cape May County in his life, the eighty-mile journey to the big city was an event to look forward to. He counted the days on his fingers. Three weeks! He wondered if he could stand it to wait that long.

He found, however, that the time went fast enough, with plenty of work to keep him busy. In the intervals of haying there were peas to be picked and fences mended. Once, toward the middle of July, they had two days of muggy, cloudy weather when Mrs. Corson decided she wanted some huckleberries to make pies.

"They ought to be just about ripe now—the high-bush ones," she told Andy at breakfast. "You an' Becky take some lunch with you an' go over to the old Townsend place. You ought to get your buckets full o' berries by afternoon."

Andy would rather have gone fishing, but at least he would get a change from hoeing and haymaking. By nine o'clock he and his sister were well up the road, each carrying a wooden milk pail.

The Townsend farm had been abandoned some years before, when a fire had burned the woodland and all of the buildings except a small log barn. It was a lonely place, well back from the road. Its northern side bordered the Gillen farm and it ran down to the marsh on the east. A few gnarled old cedar trees had escaped the fire, but most of the tract was now covered with brush and young growth taller than a man.

The boy and girl made their way through the thickets that fringed the road and quickly came to some good-sized huckleberry bushes, heavy with blue-black fruit.

"Bet you I get my bucket filled first," said Becky. She set her pail down and attacked the nearest bush with both hands.

Andy chuckled. "Sure," he replied. "You've got the small one. Mine holds two quarts more, but I'll give you a run for it at that."

With quick fingers he stripped the berries off in clusters and they drummed softly on the wooden bottom of the pail. There was no more talking. Both youngsters were intent on their contest as they moved forward, picking at top speed. Most of the time they were out of sight of each other, separated by the tall bushes, but the rustle of leaves and the ocasional snap of a twig told Andy that his sister was still close by.

After the better part of an hour the boy lifted the pail to move on to a fresh bush and noticed that the blue tide of berries had risen half way up its sides. He was about to call to Becky and boast of the fact when he heard a movement in the brush, off to his left. Then, from a scant dozen yards away, came a man's voice.

"Ain't you satisfied yet?" it whined. "Heck, Dode, I got more'n I can eat in a week, an' I'm tired."

"Go ahead an' set," another voice answered from farther away. "Take the weight off yer peg leg. Me, I aim to pick enough to sell. Hughes said he'd gimme three cents a quart, an' I'll soon have enough to buy me a bottle o' red eye. Then I s'pose you'll come around beggin' with yer tongue hangin' out, but it won't git you nowheres."

Andy had no difficulty in recognizing the voices. He knew he was listening to Dode Gowdy and his friend Stumpy, the loafers he had last seen at Enoch Hughes' store. Noiselessly he moved to his right, away from the men, and at that moment he saw Becky's face peering anxiously around a berry bush. He motioned to her to be quiet and tiptoed to her side.

"Who is it?" she whispered.

"Nobody to be scared of. Just a couple o' no-good marsh rats," he told her under his breath. "Keep still an' listen. I want to hear what they say."

They waited for what seemed a long time before there was any more conversation on the other side of the thicket. Becky peered into her brother's half-filled pail and made a face at him. He could see she was impatient to go on picking berries, but he crouched beside her, cautioning her to silence.

At last they heard Stumpy's voice again.

"When are we goin' to git some cash out o' Gillen?" he asked querulously.

Gowdy's reply was low and angry. "Shut up!" he said. "You want him to hear you?"

The one-legged man laughed. "I ain't worried 'bout that," he said. "I seen him leave. He's off shore in his garvey—prob'ly gone after hay. An' the ol' woman ain't one to gallivant around in the woods. She don't come over this way once in a 'coon's age. What we got to do is figger out a way we kin skeer him so he'll pay us."

"Yeah," Gowdy growled. "But how? If I could write I'd send him a letter without no name to it—let him know he's got to pay off if he wants us to keep our mouths shut."

"How 'bout Hughes? He's had schoolin' an' he can write good enough."

"He won't do it. I asked him. Anyhow, he's gittin' somethin' out of it himself, so why should he give a whoop about us?"

"Well, by jing!" Stumpy exclaimed. "I'll find some way to git at the ol' cuss!"

The voices had become fainter as the men talked. They seemed to be moving off in the direction of the main road. Andy heard Dode Gowdy mumble something about "better be careful," but after that they were out of earshot.

"What were they talking about?" Becky whispered, her eyes wide with excitement.

Andy shook his head. "Beats me," he said. "Sounds as if they knew something about Beasley Gillen. Something that would hurt him bad if it got out. There's a name for what they're trying to do. 'Blackmail,' I think it's called. Anyhow, it's none of our affair. Let's get these buckets filled."

They picked in silence for the next hour or two, both preoccupied with what they had heard. Finally Becky gave a little shout of triumph.

"Mine's full," she announced.

"All right, you win," Andy laughed. "I've still got

half an inch to go. Give me a hand an' we'll be through in a jiffy."

When both their pails were brimming, Becky pushed a damp curl off her forehead and fanned herself with her sunbonnet.

"Whew!" she said. "I'm hot. Let's go down to the edge of the marsh an' see if there's a breeze off the Sound."

They left the buckets under a cedar and picked their way downhill through the brush. Off to their right the roof of the little log barn looked lonely and forlorn.

Suddenly Andy stopped. The brush was thinner here, and right in front of him he saw a cart track angling up from the edge of the salt meadow. In the loose sand there were no traces of wheels or hoofs. He would have thought the trail was merely a relic of the days when the Townsends farmed the place, except for one thing. A small twig with three or four green leaves lay flattened in one of the sandy ruts, pressed down as if something heavy had passed over it.

CHAPTER VI

THAT'S FUNNY," the boy said, half to himself. "I wonder who'd use this road nowadays."

Becky was already a dozen yards ahead. "Come on," she called. "There's a southeast wind. It's cooler down here."

But Andy was still curious. He turned to the right, following the sandy cart track. It was overhung by bushes on either side, but he noticed that some of the leaves were torn. He had gone scarcely twenty paces when the road ended in a thicket.

Becky called to her brother once or twice, then came back to see why he didn't answer. To her surprise he was standing in front of a dense patch of brush, holding a juniper bough in his hand.

"Look," he said, holding the butt end toward her. "It's been cut with an ax. Somebody cut this brush and stuck it up here to look natural, so folks wouldn't come along the road."

He replaced the bough with its lower end in the sand and skirted the brush pile. As he expected, he found the road continuing a short distance beyond, and in a few more strides he came to the long-neglected yard where the farm buildings had once stood. The sand gave way to grass and weeds here, but the wheel track was easy to follow. It led directly to the old log barn.

Andy stood before the weather-beaten structure and frowned. As far as its outward appearance went, there was no sign that anyone had used it in several years. Yet there was the evidence of the cart trail, and the carefully arranged "thicket" he had found. Becky, full of curiosity as a squirrel, had darted ahead to try the old plank door of the barn.

"Look, Andy," she called. "There's a big old padlock on the door."

He joined her, staring at the heavy iron lock. It was crusted deep with rust, but the keyhole, oddly enough, was clean and open. He stepped nearer to sniff at it, and caught a faint but unmistakable odor of whale oil.

Becky strayed off to the other side of the building, trying to find a chink between the logs. It was while she was out of sight that the boy noticed a scrap of color among the straws of coarse marsh hay that were scattered about the door. Quickly he picked it up. It was a thin strip of red silk, two or three inches long. He slipped it into his pocket and turned to examine the walls of the little barn.

The fire that burned across the farm had charred the outer sides of the foot-thick logs and licked at the edges of the roof, but the structure was still solid. It even looked to Andy as if fresh mortar had been used here and there to stop up gaps in the wall.

"I wanted to see inside," said Becky with a pout, "but there aren't any windows and all the cracks are tight."

"I know," he told her. "Just the same, I'm sure somebody's been using it. Maybe this is where Gillen stores his salt hay. Never heard of anyone having to put a padlock on that stuff, though. Let's see where the road comes from."

They followed the sandy wagon track back down the hill. As Andy expected, it soon reached the edge of the marsh and skirted northward just above the salt grass. Where Beasley Gillen's land began, the trail swung to the right and they could see it led to the plank landing that thrust out on spindly piles into the Sound.

"Hey!" said Andy. "Maybe we'd better get out o' here. That looks like the garvey coming in now."

Half a mile out, her gray sail bellying in the wind, the broad-beamed barge was making slow progress toward shore. The hay piled above her gunwales gave her a shaggy, unkempt look. At her helm in the stern was a dark dot that must be Gillen's man, Jim.

The two youngsters faded back into the bushes and set out for home, picking up their berry pails on the way. Becky kept up her usual lively chatter, but she found her brother unresponsive.

"What's the matter with you today?" she asked at length. "I tell you something an' all you say is 'uh-huh.' "

"What? Oh—yeah, I was thinking, I guess. How much is silk worth a yard, Beck?"

The girl stopped in the road and stared at him as if she thought he was crazy. Then she burst out laughing.

"Silk!" she giggled. "Boys are certainly funny. But if you really want to know, it costs an awful lot. I forget how much the duty on it is, but Ma told Elvira she couldn't have a silk dress 'cause it was worth its weight in gold."

Andy nodded soberly. "That's what I thought," he said. And try as she would, Becky could get no more out of him.

He carried the problem around with him the rest of that day. It wasn't until evening, when he found his brother Luke alone, that he unburdened himself of what was on his mind.

"Luke," he whispered, "remember the piece o' red silk you found in Gillen's wagon?"

The older boy winced. "I'm not likely to forget it," he replied.

"Well, listen to this," said Andy, and he proceeded to tell about the cart track, the locked barn and the bit of red silk. Then he repeated the talk he had overheard between Stumpy and Dode Gowdy.

"I wouldn't believe it at first," he said, "an' I don't expect you to, but there's only one way it makes sense to me. Mr. Beasley Gillen's a smuggler!"

Luke whistled under his breath. "I wouldn't put it past the old stinker," he answered at last. "An' everything does add up to look that way. It's a pretty serious thing to accuse a neighbor of, though—unless you have plenty o' proof."

"I know," said Andy, frowning. "Proof is what we've got to get. I don't even want to talk to Dad about it till we're sure. But I figured with you going over there to see Prue so much, maybe you'd see some things."

"Haven't been there in a week," Luke replied with a wry grin. "An' when I do go I have to sneak around through the woods. But Prue may have some ideas, too. I'll ask her, next time I'm over that way."

Andy felt better, once he had shared his thoughts with his brother. But there was one thing he kept to himself, not mentioning it even to Luke. He couldn't escape the feeling that there was some connection between Gillen's activities and the piece of wood in his mahogany box. If he had guessed right that the carved symbols were a smugglers' code, where did the surly farmer fit in? And what about the stranger who was interested in fish hawks' nests?

Tossing on his bed that night, he tried to lay out all the facts in his mind. First there were all those trips Gillen made to Philadelphia with loads of marsh hay. He seemed to be making a lot of money out of a product that the local farmers considered almost worthless. Second there was the violent anger he had shown when Luke discovered the scrap of red silk—certainly a strange thing to find in a farm wagon. And finally it looked as if he had been hauling something from the landing and locking it up in the old Townsend barn. What could it be that needed to be hidden so carefully? Not hay, Andy was sure.

So the boy came back again to the same conclusion. Gillen must be linked up with a smuggling ring. His job was to handle goods brought ashore by smugglers, and transport them to the city.

Andy wondered what he ought to do. Until he had more definite evidence he didn't want to tell his father.

Jeremiah Corson was a man who believed in minding his own business, and he disliked meddling of any kind. Perhaps there would be an opportunity to talk it over with him on the ride to Philadelphia. And with that thought the boy gave up worrying and went to sleep.

* * *

They started cutting oats the next morning, and for three days of hot, clear weather the Corson family worked like beavers. Even Becky and Elvira were called on to rake the yellow grain into windrows and glean behind the boys as they pitched forkfuls onto the wagon. When the last load was in the barn, Andy spoke up at the supper table.

"Dad," he said, "when are we going to start for the city?"

"Let's see," his father replied. "Tomorrow's Sunday but we can use the afternoon to get ready. Ought to be able to get off early the day after, I reckon. That all right with you, Mathilda?"

"I suppose so," said Mrs. Corson. "It takes a deal o' planning to get two menfolk off on a journey, but I'll see that you're ready in time."

After church next day there was much mending and brushing of clothes, baking of bread and pies and roasting of chickens. The good woman meant to have her husband and son well fed and decent in appearance.

Andy had things to occupy him, too. When the regular chores were done he got out the currycomb and brush and went to work on the horses—his father's big gray and his own colt, Starlight. The gray had been doing farm work all summer, but plenty of grain had kept him in good condition. He looked sleek enough when the boy got through with him.

It was upon the colt that Andy really lavished his attention. Starlight's hide was black as jet, except for the four-pointed white star in the middle of his forehead. He had been out at grass most of the summer and hadn't been worked or ridden enough to keep his spirits down. Each time the boy laid the currycomb on him he danced and reared till Andy nearly lost his patience. But when at last he finished, the result was worth all the trouble it cost. The young horse gleamed like a new-polished boot.

Next Andy filled the two feed bags that would ride behind the saddles. He was working over the bridles, reins and the saddles themselves when Luke came into the barn. The older boy looked around to make sure nobody else was within hearing, then sat down on the bench beside Andy.

"I just came from Gillen's place," he whispered. "I got a word with Prue. She's scared, Andy. She didn't have time to tell me everything, but the old man beat her yesterday. She went to call him to dinner an' he was over on the Townsend farm with the team an' wagon. There was something in boxes in the wagon-bed. She couldn't tell what it was, but Gillen was covering it up with forkfuls o' hay. When he saw her over there he took a horsewhip to her!"

Luke's face was white and he clenched his fists as he spoke. "Some day," he said, "I'm going to break his neck."

Andy waited till he had calmed down a little. "What else did you hear?" he asked.

"That's about all. Gillen took off for Philadelphia yesterday afternoon. That's why I was able to see Prue. Old Jim, the colored man, isn't a bad sort, an' I guess he's sorry for her."

"Do you suppose we'll pass Gillen on the road?" Andy asked.

"I doubt it. That's a good, fast-walking team. He can make it in three days, or maybe two an' a half."

"What do the horses look like? I don't think I've ever seen 'em."

"Well," said Luke, "they're big an' well-matched for weight. One's a bay. The other's black with three white stockings. If you see a team like that, pulling a red-painted Jersey wagon, chances are it's Beasley—the dirty skunk!"

"Don't worry—I'll be watching for 'em," Andy replied. He put the finishing touches on a bridle ring and they went into the house for supper.

The Corsons' copy of the Philadelphia newspaper had arrived as usual on Friday. It was lying on a chair in the front room when Andy left the table and he picked it up to find out what might be happening in the city. It gave him an important feeling when he thought how soon he would be there himself, seeing the great world with his own eyes.

But the first item of news he read was not about Philadelphia. It struck much closer home. "Account of Action by the Revenue Cutter *Valiant* near the Delaware Capes" was the headline. And beneath it were the following paragraphs:

"We are informed through special advices, carried by the steam packet from Cape Island in New Jersey, of a spirited action which took place some leagues off Cape May on the 18th instant.

"The Revenue Cutter *Valiant,* ten guns, Lt. Craig commanding, was patrolling between the Capes of the Delaware, in search of smugglers, when a fast barque was sighted to the southeastward. The vessel was running under half sail and flying French colors. When the *Valiant* stood out to intercept her course, the barque laid on canvas and went about in evident flight. At this time the cutter was some two sea miles astern. An extremely fast sailer, she soon reduced the distance to long cannon range and signaled the barque to heave to. The signal was ignored. As the cutter drew up on the barque's starboard quarter, Lt. Craig ordered a shot from the forward nine-pounder laid across her bows. He then hailed her in the name of the U.S. Revenue Service. For answer, the French vessel threw open a row of concealed gun ports in her side, disclosing a battery of four carronades.

"The first broadside severed the cutter's topmast at the crosstrees. Her own port battery replied in kind and at least one shot was observed to take effect, entering the barque's hull close to the water line. Made unmanageable by the wreckage of her top hamper, the *Valiant* found difficulty in bringing her starboard guns to bear, and the hostile vessel seized the opportunity to run beyond cannon range. Thus the engagement was broken off, and before the damage could be repaired aboard the cutter, the suspected smuggler disappeared in a bank of fog. No wounds were reported among members of the *Valiant's* crew."

Andy's heart beat faster as he read the account. The events it described had happened almost within sight of the Cape, and he would hardly have been surprised if he had heard the rumble of cannon fire at that moment.

His eyes wandered down the page and stopped at a small advertisement. "Newly arrived," it announced, "an elegant selection of fine silks, satins, velours and laces. The Ladies of Philadelphia will be enchanted by the latest colors and fabrics from France. An especially fortunate purchase makes it possible to offer these goods at prices below the market."

The advertisement was signed by Fenimore and Groves, Chestnut Street above Third, "at the Sign of the Shears."

It was the word "silks" that had first caught his attention. The reference to low prices added to his interest. If he should chance to be in the neighborhood of Third and Chestnut, he thought he might look for the "Sign of the Shears."

He packed his saddlebags before he went to bed that evening, for they planned an early start. His mother had already gone upstairs but he found his father in the kitchen, hard at work cleaning something with an oily cloth.

"Can't tell what we'll meet on the roads," Jeremiah Corson remarked with a grin. "I reckon we may as well take this with us."

And as he laid aside the rag, Andy saw that he held a long-barreled horse pistol in his hand.

CHAPTER VII

NOBODY HAD TO CALL the boy that Monday morning. He was awake when the first rooster crowed, long before daybreak. By sunrise he and his father had eaten breakfast and were saddling the horses.

The farmer grumbled a little as he strapped the heavy food box on the gray's rump. "You'd think," he said, "from the amount o' food your Ma has given us we might be headed for Ohio."

"That's right," Andy laughed. "I saw her pack it. There's two whole chickens an' five loaves o' bread, besides cheese an' pickles an' half a ham an' two mince pies. One thing's sure—we won't have to buy many meals in taverns along the way!"

The family came out to see them off. Mr. Corson gave the older boys some parting advice about the farm work, and he and Andy in turn were showered with reminders by the womenfolk. At last the good-byes were said and they rode out of the yard. When Andy looked back, the last thing he saw was old Shep standing by the gate, his tail wagging slowly and wistfully.

It was as fine a morning as any traveler could ask. There was dew twinkling on the grass and the air was cool and clear. The early sunlight glittered on the surface of the Sound. The roadside cedars rustled in the breeze, and overhead a big gray osprey went flapping sturdily seaward.

The colt was full of ginger and eager for a run, and it was all Andy could do to hold him in. As the young horse chafed at the bit, flecks of foam from his mouth drifted back to stain his satiny black shoulders.

"Feeling mighty fine, isn't he?" the older man chuckled. "Just wait a few hours till we hit those soft sand roads up in the pines. He'll settle down."

So they jogged northward past the neighbors' farms,

commenting on the stands of corn and the state of fields and fences as they rode along. By nine o'clock they had left their own part of the county and were entering Upper Township. They passed the Little Quaker Meeting House and the cluster of houses at Seaville, then swung to the left off the main Shore Road and cut through the woods on a rutted sandy track that led toward Tuckahoe.

Half a dozen times in the course of the morning they came to streams that had to be forded. And once there was a broad tidal creek where they waited half an hour for a flatboat to come from the other shore and ferry them across.

It was nearing noon when they rode into Tuckahoe. Aside from a sad-faced hound dog that sat scratching himself in the middle of the road, and a farm team hitched in front of the village store, the place seemed to be sound asleep.

"May as well get across the river 'fore we stop to eat," Jeremiah Corson said. "If the bridge is in decent shape, that is."

They paid their toll of a penny apiece to the drowsy gatekeeper and walked the horses across the rickety-looking structure that spanned the Tuckahoe River. In the shade of a big oak on the northern bank they dismounted. Bread, ham and cheese from the food box made them a good lunch, and half a mile farther up the road they picked up some early apples and got a drink at a farmyard well.

During the morning the wind had shifted easterly. The sky began clouding over as they rode northward. Twenty-five miles of steady going had taken some of the wildness out of the black colt, and Andy found him manageable enough as he plodded through the sand behind the other horse.

They were in the deep woods now. As the sky grew darker overhead the cart trail became dim and shadowy. Once the colt shied a little, and Andy was startled by a glimpse of a gray fox crouching by the edge of the road. It vanished almost before he knew what it was, slipping silently off into the brush.

The boy was glad of his father's big solid back, up there ahead. This was a lonely stretch of country, and it seemed a long way from home. The gloominess of the day increased toward midafternoon when rain began to fall. It started gently, but by the time they forded Stephens Creek a steady drizzle was coming down. They pulled up in the shelter of a pine tree and put on the slickers which had been strapped under their saddle cantles.

An hour later they crossed the log bridge over South River.

"Don't get discouraged, boy," Jeremiah Corson called over his shoulder. "We're not so far from the

Great Egg now. Ought to get to May's Landing by five o'clock if we keep right at it."

"Are we going to sleep there?" Andy asked. "It'll be dark early tonight."

"No, I'd planned to push along to Weymouth. That's nearer the halfway mark to Philadelphia."

Another two miles brought them to the side of the Great Egg River, gray and misty in the rain. There were several sailing vessels moored in the roadstead and ship-ways stood along the bank, for May's Landing was the head of tidewater on the river. In spite of the downpour, Andy looked about him with a thrill of excitement as they rode on into the village. This was the largest town he had ever been in. There must be more than a hundred buildings, including a courthouse more pretentious than the one in Cape May County, several churches and a number of fine mansions built by well-to-do sea captains.

At the tavern where they stopped to rest the horses and dry their clothes, the stage from Camden was just pulling in. Andy saw four or five travelers climb stiffly out of the mud-spattered vehicle and make their way to the inn parlor. Potboys hurried out to bring their luggage from the deep leather "boot" at the back of the coach, while hostlers came from the stable to take charge of the four weary horses. Last of all the driver, a lordly figure in his great oilskin coat and wide-brimmed hat, furled his whip and stalked into the taproom.

The country lad was so fascinated by all this commotion that he paid little heed to the conversation going on beside him. His father was talking to the proprietor of the tavern, a man named Jenkins who came from their own Middle Township. Suddenly a name was mentioned that caught Andy's attention.

"Calls himself Beasley Gillen," the innkeeper was saying. "I've known Beasleys all my life, but he's new to me. Neighbor o' yours, ain't he? Stops in here every few weeks, haulin' to the city an' back. I'd say he's mighty prosperous—leastways, he always pays in hard cash an' seems to have plenty of it."

Mr. Corson nodded. "So I've heard," he replied noncommittally. "He's not one to talk much, an' I've never inquired into his affairs."

They changed the subject after that, but Andy couldn't help wondering if any of the inn servants had ever poked under the loads of marsh hay on the farmer's Jersey wagon.

After half an hour Jeremiah Corson pulled on his slicker once more. "Time to be going, son," he remarked. "We'd better get on our way while there's still some daylight."

Andy brought the horses around from the stable and they remounted, splashing out of town through mud that was fetlock deep. They passed a gristmill and skirted the pond above the dam, then plunged into the half-darkness of thick woods.

It was less than six miles to Weymouth, but the road was so bad they found it difficult to move faster than a walk. In the dusk Andy could barely see his father's bulky shape, hunched against the storm. They had been traveling close to an hour when the gray horse stumbled. He went halfway to his knees but caught himself and stood trembling, his head hanging down. Andy ranged up alongside as his father swung out of the saddle.

"What happened?" the boy asked. "Did he trip over a root?"

Jeremiah Corson didn't answer at once. He was stooping to feel the horse's forelegs, running his hand from ankle to knee. Finally he stood up.

"Doesn't seem to be in the tendons," he said. "But he's tender in that off leg. Something's hurting him bad."

He took the bridle and tried to lead the gray forward. The horse made a limping stride or two and stopped again.

Andy dismounted. "S'pose it could be the hoof?" he asked.

His father reached down and took hold of the right forefoot just above the pastern. "Come, boy," he urged gently. "Pick up your foot."

As the horse's knee bent he lifted the hoof, peering at its underside in the darkness, then set it down again. "Can't see a thing," he growled disgustedly, "an' we're miles from the nearest light."

"Wait, Dad," Andy murmured. "You're wrong about that. Look there."

Among the trees they saw a flickering gleam. Then a man stepped out into the road, holding a pine-knot torch above his head. The flames wavered and hissed in the rain, but they were bright enough to light up the most terrifying figure Andy had ever seen. The man was broad and squat, with a great ragged beard, and he seemed to be black from head to foot. As he came closer the boy could see streaks of lighter color in the dark mask of his face. For a moment he wished fervently that his father's horse pistol was within reach.

"What's wrong?" asked the stranger in a gruff voice.

"Horse went lame," Jeremiah Corson replied. "If you'll be kind enough to hold your light here, maybe we can tell why."

He sounded so calm and unconcerned that Andy was ashamed of his own fright. The bearded man brought the torch nearer, and again Corson lifted the gray's forefoot.

"Steady there, boy," he murmured. "I can see it now."

Andy saw it, too. A rough object like a small stone

was wedged between the hoof wall and the tender "frog." His father's strong fingers worked at it for a moment and pulled it free.

"Looks like a piece o' slag," he said, holding it to the light. "Sharp edges. No wonder it hurt him."

The big horse set his foot gingerly on the ground, tested his weight on it and sighed gratefully.

"We're mighty obliged to you," Andy's father told the stranger. "I reckon you're a charcoal burner. Lucky for us you chanced to be so handy."

"My shack's right yonder, 'bout a musket shot," the man replied. "Come over an' dry out if you've a mind. The kiln's goin' an' I was outside tendin' it."

"We'll stop a few minutes, an' thank you kindly," said the farmer. "If Mr. Colwell's at the Iron Works we'll go on there to spend the night."

They followed the torch a short distance into the woods and came into a clearing where there was a small log cabin, a big stack of pine cordwood and what looked like a cone-shaped pile of sand a dozen feet high. They tied the horses in the lee of the shack and Jeremiah Corson went inside. Andy, who had never seen charcoal made, stayed with the sooty-faced burner to see how it was done.

There was a steady outpouring of smoke from the top of the cone, and every now and then it was tinged with a reddish glow. Moving around to the front of the kiln, the boy saw a brighter spot of red close to the ground. That, the charcoal burner told him, was the draft hole. At each burning he built up a pile of wood, broad at the base and narrowing toward the top. This was covered with turf on all sides, then with sand to make it airtight. The only openings were the vent at the peak and the draft hole at the bottom. Once the wood was set afire it had to be kept burning slowly and evenly for several days.

"What happens then?" Andy asked the bearded man.

"Have to let it cool a spell. Then I bust up the kiln an' pull the charcoal out, careful-like. It's brittle stuff. Here—this piece'll show you."

From the ground he picked up a foot-long black stick and snapped it between his fingers before handing it to the boy.

"Good charcoal's mighty near pure carbon," he explained. "All I make goes to the furnace to make iron. They send down wagons once a week an' haul off what I've burned. It ain't the cleanest job in the world but it's a livin'."

Twenty minutes later the Corsons were back on the road once more. The rain had slackened, but night was close upon them.

"Must be suppertime," said Andy's father. "My stomach says so, anyway."

"What sort of a place is Weymouth?" the boy asked.

"Pretty good-sized place. Five or six hundred folks live here, I reckon. Back a few years, in wartime, it was mighty busy, too. Made cannon an' cannonballs that helped us whip the British. Now I guess it's iron pipe, mostly. They get their iron out o' the bogs up above here, an' there's plenty o' pine timber to make charcoal, so it's a natural place for a furnace an' forge."

Even as he finished speaking they saw the first lights of the village ahead. The road widened and the horses stepped out more eagerly, smelling supper and a stable close at hand.

To their right rose the tall brick tower of the blast furnace. The fiery glare from its top shed an eerie red light over the trees and houses. The glare seemed to come and go at regular intervals, and a deep panting sound came from the giant leather bellows, driven by a waterwheel, that forced air upward through the furnace.

They pulled up at the hitching rail in front of a two-story frame house where candlelight shone behind the wet windowpanes. A moment later Jeremiah Corson was being warmly greeted at the door. Charles Colwell, the ironmaster, stood there smiling, his napkin in his hand.

"You and the boy are just in time to eat with us,

Jem," he said. "I'll have my stableman take care o' the horses."

They protested that they had plenty of food with them, but Colwell refused to listen. "You've had a long day's ride in the rain," he said. "What you need is a hot meal by a good fire. Come in here, now."

That was an evening Andy wouldn't forget for a long time. A delicious supper, warmth and good cheer made up for all the discomfort of the afternoon. He heard story after story about the grim days of 1812 to 1815, and the night-and-day labor that had produced desperately needed guns.

At nine o'clock Andy's father got up from his comfortable chair by the fire. "Bedtime for us travelers, Charlie," he grinned. "We'll have to get up early if we want to reach Philadelphia tomorrow."

CHAPTER VIII

THE RAIN WAS OVER when they woke at dawn, and the wind was back in the northwest. They set off as soon as they'd breakfasted. The gray horse had completely recovered from the lameness caused by the lump of slag in his hoof, and he stepped out as willingly as the colt.

As soon as they crossed Weymouth bridge they found the road better. It was in constant use by the broad-wheeled wagons that hauled finished iron forgings and castings north to the city. They passed one an hour after they started. It was a massive, low-bodied rig, loaded with lengths of heavy water pipe. The driver cracked his twenty-foot whip, and three pairs of mules strained at the tugs as they pulled through mudholes left by the rain.

Half a mile farther on they overtook another wagon with a similar cargo, and before the morning was over they had counted six more. The Weymouth Iron Works was still doing a big business.

That wasn't the only traffic on the highway. They passed slow-moving droves of cattle and pigs headed for market, and red Jersey wagons piled with produce. At the Blue Anchor Tavern, which they reached in mid-forenoon, a Camden-bound stage was changing horses. It came up behind them half an hour later, the team at a gallop and the horn sounding to clear the way.

Starlight caught the excitement and wanted to race the coach, but Andy's father forbade it.

"We'll be there tonight, soon as they are," the farmer told his son. "With relays every fifteen or twenty miles, they can afford to burn up the roads. But the stops they make for meals an' changing teams use up all the time they gain. Just wait an' see. We'll catch up to 'em."

By that time they were out of the pines and moving

through well-cleared farming country. They ate their lunch beside a pond near the village of Long-a-Coming. The stage, which had stopped for nooning at an inn in the little town, came rattling past as they prepared to get into their saddles again.

"All right," Andy's father grinned, "our horses have had a rest, an' we're near enough to let 'em out a bit if you want."

So they cantered after the coach as it swung into Haddonfield, passed it when it made a stop at the Indian Queen, and were well ahead as they entered the outskirts of Camden. Off to his left, Andy could see Windmill Island and the white sails of great merchant ships on the Delaware. And beyond the broad river was the city of Philadelphia itself!

For the country boy from Cape May that was a great moment. He was looking at the most important place on the North American continent, the first capital of the young nation and still its greatest town, in spite of the rapid growth of New York, to the north. Andy could hardly wait to cross over and set foot on its famous streets.

But wait he did. When they reached the ferry wharf the boat had just pulled out and was chugging into the stream, a great cloud of black smoke pouring from its stack. They got off their horses and stood there watching it as it angled across the river against a strong tide.

The sun was setting when the ferry returned, an hour later. Jeremiah Corson paid their fares and they led the horses aboard, hitching them to rings along the rail. Another rider, a Jersey wagon, and a dozen people on foot made up the rest of the load. When the bell clanged and the paddles began to churn, it was too much for Starlight. The colt snorted and reared. Andy caught his bridle, pulled him down and calmed him with quiet words while the craft nosed out into the Delaware.

"Don't blame him a mite," the farmer said. "I don't like these contraptions either. Liable to blow up any minute. The boats they used to have were a lot safer, even if they weren't as big or as fast. They ran by horsepower, on a treadmill. Every horse that came aboard had to work his way across."

In spite of Mr. Corson's dire predictions, the steam vessel made the crossing safely, and was tied up to the wharf on the Philadelphia side. Even at that hour of the early evening the waterfront was bustling with activity. Half a dozen tall ships were moored along the docks, and their cargo was being unloaded with much singing and shouting by a swarm of stevedores. Big drays loaded with merchandise went rattling over the cobbles. Scattered among the great dark warehouses were little waterfront shops where lights were beginning to shine behind the counters.

Andy and his father remounted and rode up the steep slope of Market Street. It was a wide thoroughfare, unlighted except for such rays from lamps and candles as came through the small-paned windows. The few pedestrians on the street carried pierced tin lanterns to light their way.

When they reached Front Street, at the top of the hill, they passed the long sheds of the farmers' market, set in the middle of the highway. They were dark now, for the buying and selling were over for the day.

At Fourth Street the travelers swung northward and rode past Mulberry and Cherry, to Sassafras Street. There, at the Moon and Seven Stars Inn, they entered a courtyard and turned the horses over to a stable boy. Jeremiah Corson had stopped here before and knew the innkeeper. They were served a good supper in the dining room that adjoined the bar, then shown to a bedroom on the second floor, where their saddlebags had already been carried.

"What I like about this place," said Andy's father, "is the beds. Most inns, you get a shuck mattress. Here they put you on a real featherbed."

It was a hot night and Andy privately wished the feather mattress had not been so soft and stifling. But he was tired enough from the long ride to sleep soundly in spite of any discomfort.

The sound that woke him was unfamiliar but pleasant. It was a mellow Negro voice, calling something that was half a song. It took several repetitions of the words for his drowsy mind to make any sense out of them.

"Come an' git yo' pepperpot—full o' meat an' smoky hot!" sang the voice.

Andy crawled out of the bed, where his father still lay asleep. From the window he looked down on the pavement. A big, jolly-looking woman with a red kerchief tied over her head was holding a steaming copper kettle. As he watched, a housewife came out of the door of the house opposite. She was holding a stew-pan into which the Negress poured a quart of hot, thick liquid. "Pepperpot," the boy gathered, must be some kind of soup.

He put on his clothes and stole out without waking his father. When he reached the street he found the early morning air was cool and fresh. On Sassafras Street, sometimes called Race Street because the town's younger gentry tested the speed of their horses there, traffic was already moving. Farmers' carts, coming down the Ridge Pike from Germantown and other outlying villages, were on their way to the market stalls. Clerks and apprentices hurried by, anxious to be at work by six.

Andy walked south toward the heart of the city. He

stared goggle-eyed at the great buildings, three and four stories high and built of brick. Occasionally he stood on tiptoe to look over garden walls at tiny plots of green grass, elaborate flower beds and neatly pruned fruit trees. He wondered what it would be like to live in a city, hemmed in by brick and stone. No, he decided—a few days' visit would be about all he could stand.

After strolling three or four squares he went back to the tavern. The faded blue sign, painted with a crescent moon and seven stars, creaked gently in the morning breeze. And from the open door came an appetizing smell of broiling bacon. His father was up and dressed, waiting for him in the dining room.

When they had finished breakfast, Jeremiah Corson outlined the day's business. "First off," he said, "we must get that suit o' clothes ordered. There's a Quaker named Matlack, on Chestnut Street, who tailors good solid stuff at a fair price. After that I'll go an' attend to some legal matters an' you can look around a bit. Here's half a dollar for spending money, an' see you don't squander it on trash."

They walked up Sassafras to Seventh, then south across Market till they came to Chestnut Street. There were numerous shops in the neighborhood, though the residences of wealthy townsfolk still dominated the street. A modest sign announced the tailoring establishment of Aaron Matlack. Inside, the proprietor greeted them and brought several bolts of heavy woolen cloth for inspection. After some discussion, Mr. Corson chose a serviceable dark blue broadcloth for his son's suit. Andy was measured, and the coat and pantaloons were promised for delivery next day.

The boy wanted brass buttons, but his father vetoed the idea. "You'll look enough like a sailor as it is," he remarked. "Besides, if you lose a brass button where are you? Bone ones are easier to come by, down our way."

When they had left the shop and Andy was on his own, he had a hard time deciding what to see first. But a glance down Chestnut Street toward the tower of the State House made up his mind. With a quickened heartbeat he set off for a closer view of the most famous building in America.

He wasn't disappointed. The mellow red brick structure with its flanking buildings had all the stately grace he had dreamed of. Hesitating to enter from the front, he walked down Sixth Street till he came to a gate in the low brick wall. It stood open and he went in.

At first he thought there was no one else in the garden. Then he saw an old man in a leather apron kneeling among the flower beds, and approached him, hat in hand.

"Excuse me," the boy said, "but is it all right for me to walk in here?"

"Why not?" asked the old gardener testily. "American, ain't ye?"

"Yes," said Andy.

"Well, it's yours, then. 'For the use an' pleasure o' the American people forever'—that's the law."

Andy watched a little while as the man worked with patient fingers among the flowers. "You know this place well, I guess?" he asked at length.

"Should say I do!" the old fellow snorted. "Been workin' around here since Mr. Vaughan planted these elm trees, in 'eighty-five. An' way before that, when I was just a lad, I heard the bell ring out fer Independence, back in July o' 'seventy-six. Yes, I reckon I know the place better'n most. Go on in. There'll be nobody to stop ye."

The boy went slowly along the flagstone walks and up to the door that opened on the garden. There was a cool mustiness inside, and his footsteps echoed in the silence. He passed the staircases leading to the floor above and found himself in a spacious central hall, with a wide door opening off either side. Now that the Pennsylvania capital had been moved inland to Harrisburg the old building was little used, and it seemed to Andy to be falling into decay. In the handsome room on his right, where the Declaration had been signed, there was thick dust on the chairs and the paint was flaking off the door and window frames.

Reverently he went about the room, standing with bared head before the platform where Washington had sat, trying to picture other great men of that assemblage. It was too bad, he thought, that Americans of his own day cared so little about the past. He wondered if the State House would be left to crumble away, or torn down to make room for a more modern building.

His feeling of sadness had left him by the time he was out on the sunny pavement once more. It was too fine a day to worry about old landmarks. He walked on down Chestnut Street past Fifth and Fourth, headed for no place in particular. And then, a hundred yards in front of him, he saw a pair of horses come out of an alley. A stable boy had them by their halters and was leading them to the watering trough at the edge of the street. Andy had seen plenty of horses since coming to the big town, but one of these caught his eye. It was a big black drafter with one foreleg that was white halfway to the knee, and two more white "stockings" behind. When they dropped their heads to drink thirstily, he saw that the other horse was a powerful bay.

The Jersey boy breathed faster as he approached. He slowed his step and loitered near the water trough.

"Whose team is that?" he asked, trying to sound casual.

The young hostler looked him up and down with a supercilious eye. "Dunno's it's any o' your affair—Piney!" He accompanied the word with a squirt of tobacco juice that barely missed Andy's foot. "What you wanna know for? Thinkin' o' buyin' 'em?"

His jeering laugh made Andy flush and double his fists. He had a sharp answer on the tip of his tongue but he bit it back. It wasn't likely that fighting would help him find out what he needed to know. He stepped back and looked into the alley. There was a stable at the end of it, and he could see the rear wheels and part of the body of a Jersey wagon standing inside.

That was proof enough for Andy. He walked past the big team and the stable boy without giving them another glance. He was looking for something else now, and near the corner of the next cross street he saw it. It was a two-story building with an ornate sign hanging over the door. The painting of a huge pair of shears on the sign made it hardly necessary for him to read the gilt letters underneath—"FENIMORE & GROVES, Drapers."

He went to the window of the shop and looked in through the small, square panes. It was dark inside, and he had been walking eastward, into the sun. It took a moment or two for his eyes to adjust themselves. Then he saw a display of dress goods, arranged to catch the attention of passing ladies. There were velvets, satins and brocades, but the material he looked at longest was none of these. It was rich red silk of a shade he had seen only once before in his life.

CHAPTER IX

ANDY STAYED AT THE WINDOW a long time, staring at the scarlet silk. There were more and more people on the street now. Fashionable ladies in giddy bonnets, prosperous, beaver-hatted businessmen and young dandies wearing the latest in tight fawn-colored pantaloons, bright waistcoats and high-collared coats came strolling by. Some of them looked at the gangling boy in his country clothes and laughed.

At first he was too much absorbed to be conscious of their amusement, but after a while their remarks began to nettle him. Until that moment he hadn't realized how his homespun jeans and cowhide boots set him apart from these city dwellers. With an added tinge of red under his sunburn, he turned and walked eastward down the slope that led toward the river.

Off to his right was Dock Creek. Rows of shallops and fishing boats with masts leaning at all angles lay tied to the rickety piers. It was low tide, and the smell of mud flats along the creek made him a little homesick.

He kept on till he reached the riverbank, where he spent the rest of the morning watching the ships being loaded and unloaded. At noon he went into a waterside tavern with sanded floors and found a seat at a corner table. Wanting to try Philadelphia pepperpot he ordered a big bowl of it, along with bread, cheese and a wedge of apple pie. It made a good meal and a filling one, though he thought the price they charged was rather high. In all, it came to fourteen cents.

Later he moved slowly northward from dock to dock. He saw the warehouses and square-rigged ships of the famous merchant, Stephen Girard. For an hour or more he watched hopefully for a glimpse of the great man himself, but Girard must have been occupied with affairs elsewhere that day.

At the edge of the Northern Liberties he climbed the riverbank and found himself in a great, wide road that stretched westward between pleasant houses and rows of trees. Inquiring at a market stall he was told it was called Spring Garden Street, which seemed to him a pretty name. He followed it to Fourth, where he turned south and made his way back to the Moon and Seven Stars.

The afternoon was nearly done when he reached the tavern. He found his father going over some papers in their room and gave him an account of his day.

"Dad," he said finally, "there's something I've been wanting to talk to you about. If you were sure there was smuggling going on, an' had a good idea who was doing it, what would you do?"

Jeremiah Corson looked at him in some surprise. "Why, report 'em to the authorities, I guess. I know there's a lot o' folks think smuggling isn't so bad, but the law's the law. Way I look at it, a smuggler's stealing from the Government. Stealing from me, too, because I vote an' pay taxes. But the main thing is, it's law-breaking. An' that makes it just as wrong as robbery or murder. You better tell me what's on your mind, son."

Andy started at the beginning. He told his father about the talk he had heard at the store between Dode Gowdy and Stumpy, and how he had connected it with the schooner he had seen coming from Townsend's Inlet.

"I reckon it was their crew that killed our heifer," he said. "But if they were setting smuggled goods ashore, I couldn't figure who was working with 'em on land. Then I remembered Beasley Gillen coming out in his garvey the night before."

His father shook his head. "That's sort of a hasty guess," he told the boy. "Gillen isn't much of a neighbor, it's true, but he minds his business an' makes out all right as a farmer."

"I know," said Andy. "Sometimes it seems as if he made out too well. All those trips o' his up here to the city, hauling marsh hay—how does he make it pay? But that isn't all, Dad. Listen to this."

He went on to tell about the scrap of red silk Luke had found in the bottom of the Jersey wagon, though he omitted any mention of the pitchfork incident.

"Then," he said, "less'n a week ago Becky an' I were berrying on the old Townsend place. Gowdy an' Stumpy were there in the brush, too. They didn't see us, but we could hear 'em talking good an' plain. They were trying to figure some way to make Gillen pay 'em for keeping their mouths shut about what he's doing."

He recounted the conversation word for word, and as he talked he could see his father's face grow grim.

"Afterwards," he went on, "Beck an' I went on down near the marsh where the farm buildings used to be. The old log barn's still there an' it's been fixed up—chinked an' made tight. There's a padlock on the door, too, an' a wagon track up to it from Gillen's landing. He's keeping something there an' I bet it isn't marsh hay. Right in front o' the barn door I picked up a bit of red silk!"

He waited for his father to comment, but all he said was, "Go ahead. Let's hear the rest."

"Well," the boy continued, "today I found a shop on Chestnut Street where they were showing that same shade o' bright red silk in the window. An' just a few steps away, at a stable in the alley, I saw Beasley Gillen's team an' wagon."

Jeremiah Corson stretched out his legs, put his hands behind his head and looked thoughtfully at the ceiling.

"Looks as if you'd made out quite a case," he remarked at length. "I'm not a lawyer, but if I was, I b'lieve I could convince a jury with all that evidence. As it is, about all we can do is keep our eyes peeled an' get ready to talk to the sheriff or the revenue men if we find out anything more. I'm glad you told me, Andy. But let's keep it to ourselves for now."

After supper that evening they went out to see what entertainment the city had to offer. It was a fine night, cooler than the previous one, and hundreds of people were strolling the pavements. On Walnut Street they found a crowd moving westward. Two or three squares away they could see flares lighting the sky and there was a sound of lively music.

Jeremiah Corson asked a passer-by what the attraction might be.

"Coletti's open-air circus," the man replied. "I ain't been to see it yet, but they do say it's a spectacle. Acrobats an' elephants an' a genuwine man-eatin' Bengal tiger."

The two Jerseymen followed the crowd to the vacant lot where the circus was in progress. Inside a high canvas fence, rows of torches illuminated the colorful scene. Signor Coletti, in person, was the ringmaster. He wore a gold-frogged red coat, white breeches and shiny black boots, and Andy thought he made the finest figure he had ever seen.

When he cracked his whip a fat white horse trotted into the ring and a golden-haired lady in a shockingly brief skirt sprang to its back. Amid loud applause she stood erect, pirouetted and did a handstand while the horse ambled around the ring. An act featuring several performing dogs followed. Then came the acrobats, and finally a vast, shadowy gray thing shuffled into the circle of light. Andy's eyes nearly popped from their sockets. He had heard that elephants were big, but this animal was so enormous he could scarcely believe it. He watched, breathless, while the elephant waltzed ponderously in time to the music, lifted a barrel with its trunk, and did other astonishing things.

When the huge beast was led out of the ring, the appearance of the "man-eating Bengal tiger" was a disappointment. It lay on the floor of a cage, looking mangy and unhappy, and it wasn't much larger than old Shep, the collie.

At the end of the show the Corsons went back to their inn. Andy was too full of all he had seen to be sleepy. He lay there in the featherbed for hours, wide-awake. He heard the ringing call of the night watch: "Eleven o'clock of a fine, clear night—eleven o'clock an' all's well!" And he heard it again at midnight. When he finally did drop off to sleep his dreams were crowded with the fantastic shapes of circus animals.

As a consequence he slept late next morning. His father was up and shaving at the washstand when he finally woke, and the sounds of the street told him the day must be well started.

"Better hustle up an' dress," Jeremiah Corson urged. "If they've got your suit done we could make a start for home by noon."

After breakfast they revisited Matlack's tailoring establishment and found Andy's clothes nearly finished. He tried on the coat and admired its smooth cut in the tall mirror at the back of the shop.

"It'll be half an hour before we've put the last touches to it," the tailor told them. "Take a walk around the town and I'll have it ready when you come back."

Andy led his father eastward, down Chestnut Street.

"I guess you've seen the State House before," he said. "But maybe you'd like to take a look at that stable where I saw the team."

When they reached the alley between Fourth and Third, the boy went straight in. With his father behind him he stopped at the stable door and looked inside. The wagon was gone. "Mr. Gillen gone?" he asked the stable boy.

The youth was about to give him a scornful answer, but the sight of the big farmer made him change his mind.

"Yeah," he replied. "He left first thing this mornin'."

Andy walked in, passing the rows of stalls, the feed boxes and haymows. The stable was a long building, stretching eastward from the alley for more than a hundred feet. Far at the rear he found what he was looking for—a small door in the north wall. He tried to open it but it was locked or bolted from the other side. Turning, he paced off the distance carefully. It was forty steps back to the alley.

"What's that for?" asked his father.

"I'll show you in a minute," Andy said. Then he turned and faced the stable boy who had started to follow them out of the alley.

"We don't want your company," he told him evenly. "If you know what's good for you you'll stay right here."

Sullenly the young hostler returned to the stable door. At the street, Andy turned east once more and began counting. Forty paces brought him to a point squarely in front of the Sign of the Shears.

"That's the way I figured," he said. "There must be a back door to this shop that opens right into the stable. That makes it mighty easy for 'em to bring in smuggled goods."

He beckoned to his father to come closer to the window and showed him the length of red silk displayed there. After a thoughtful moment Jeremiah Corson nodded, his face grave.

"Looks as if you might be right," he told the boy. "There's no actual proof, o' course, but it looks suspicious." He hesitated, stroking his chin. "Tell you what," he said, coming to a decision. "You go along back to the tailor's, an' I'll be there after a bit."

Andy was full of curiosity but it didn't seem like a time for asking questions. Obediently he set off up Chestnut Street. When he reached the corner and looked back, his father was out of sight.

The new suit was wrapped in a neat bundle, ready to be taken out, when he got to Matlack's shop, but it was more than half an hour before Jeremiah Corson arrived. He paid the bill and they started back to their lodgings.

"I reckon you've been wondering where I went,"

said Andy's father as they walked along Seventh Street. "I remembered that I used to know a lawyer named Sedley. He's Collector o' the Port now, an' I figured he'd be interested in smugglers. So I went down to the Custom House an' talked to him. Seems he's had some suspicions himself about those silks at Fenimore an' Groves. He's going to keep a watch on the stable, an' he suggests we get in touch with the commander o' the revenue cutter, down Cape May way. Fellow named Craig—a lieutenant, I believe."

"Gosh!" Andy exclaimed. "I've read about him in the paper. His cutter's the *Valiant*—ten guns. Jesse said she comes into Dennis Creek every week or two, an' he's acquainted with some o' the crew!"

It was nearly noon when they reached the tavern. Andy's father gave orders for the horses to be saddled while they packed their bags and ate an early lunch. By two o'clock they had made the ferry crossing and were jogging along by Cooper's Creek. The horses were fresh and eager. On level ground they were allowed to go at a canter, and they covered the fifteen miles to Long-a-Coming in less than two hours.

"Where do you think we'll be by night?" Andy asked.

"Well," his father replied, "I'd expected to stop over at Blue Anchor, but it looks like we'll do better'n that. It's going to be a good clear night an' I reckon it wouldn't hurt us to sleep out, if we don't happen to be near an inn."

It was nearing six o'clock when they rode past the Blue Anchor Tavern. Among the vehicles standing in the wide innyard Andy saw a red Jersey wagon that looked familiar, and he pulled the colt to a stop. At that moment a short, thickset man came out of the stable. As he tramped across the yard, the boy had a good glimpse of his face, scowling and truculent. Andy didn't wait to be recognized. He touched his heel to Starlight's side and rode on after his father.

"Gillen's back there," he reported, when the colt had overtaken the gray. "Stopped at the tavern for the night, I guess."

"Hmm," his father replied. "That's a good thing, maybe. We'll be home ahead of him, an' I'd sort o' like to look around the old Townsend barn while he isn't there."

They were well down the road to Weymouth before darkness fell. Jeremiah Corson picked a grassy spot beside a small stream for their camping place and they unsaddled the horses, letting them drink and roll. When they had been grained and tethered for the night, Andy and his father ate some of the provisions that remained in the food box and settled down under the trees. The pine needles made a clean, firm bed, more comfortable, to Andy's way of thinking, than the feather mattress at the inn. He fell asleep to the chuckling sound of the brook and didn't wake till dawn.

It was only a few miles to Weymouth Forge, and they had breakfast there at the ironmaster's house. By eight o'clock they were on the road again. Soon May's Landing was behind them, and the South River ford. When they crossed the bridge into Tuckahoe, early in the afternoon, the tired horses pricked up their ears and moved more eagerly.

"Must be the smell o' salt marsh," Andy's father commented. "They know they're in Cape May County now."

Andy had the same feeling. It seemed as if he had been away a long time. And when the farmhouse came in sight, a little before sunset, he wanted to shout and yell. Instead, he rode into the yard at a sedate pace, as an experienced traveler should. He swung stiffly out of the saddle and was nearly knocked off his feet by old Shep's welcome. He was home again.

CHAPTER X

THERE WAS A SHRIEK and a clatter from the kitchen and Becky came racing out, her pigtails flying. "Mom!" she cried. "It's Dad an' Andy!"

Mrs. Corson followed, drying her hands on her apron, and after her came Elvira. Then the boys appeared, hurrying from the barn.

"Laws-a-mercy!" Andy's mother exclaimed. "You

must've come a-flying. We didn't expect you for another day!"

"Not going to starve us, are you—just because we're early?" Jeremiah Corson asked with mock sternness, and the whole family laughed at the idea.

They unbuckled their saddlebags and Jess and Luke led the horses off to the barn. Andy and his father were dusty from the long day's ride. They washed up before supper, then sat down with the others at a table loaded with good things.

Jeremiah Corson bowed his head. "We thank thee, Father," he said reverently, "for the food we are about to eat, for thy blessing on this house, an' for our safe homecoming. Amen."

There was a rapid fire of questions from the girls while they ate. What did Andy think of the big city? Did he get his new clothes? What were the ladies wearing on Chestnut Street? (That was Elvira.) And did they have any adventures with robbers? (That was Becky.)

Andy did most of the answering, for he was full of the wonders he had seen. He told them about the State House, the circus elephant and the ships. After supper he put on his suit for his mother and the girls to admire. It was bedtime before he had a chance to talk to Luke alone. Then he gave him the news about Beasley Gillen, the stable, and the silk in the window at the Sign of the Shears.

"Finally," he told him, "I couldn't hold back any longer an' told Dad the whole thing. He sort of pooh-poohed the idea at first, but he believes it now. He even talked to the customs collector before we started home—an' he's going to see the commander o' that cutter in the bay!"

"Gee!" Luke whispered. "Maybe there'll be some excitement 'round here! All I want is to be in the posse that goes in to get ol' Gillen!"

"Any word from Prudence?" Andy asked.

"No. I've been over that way twice, but Gillen's wife must be watching her sharper'n ever."

They went to bed then, and before Andy knew it, it was morning—time to get up and do the early chores.

"Seeing's we're home a day ahead o' time," his father remarked at breakfast, "I'll let you two older boys carry on with the work. Andy an' I have got some business to attend to this morning."

Andy could see that Becky was almost bursting with curiosity, but a warning glance from him helped her keep it bottled up. When Jess and Luke had gone to the fields and the womenfolk started on the housework, the boy and his father went outside.

"Might as well walk," said Jeremiah Corson. "We don't want to attract too much attention."

They went up the road, stopping once or twice to pass the time of day with neighboring farmers. It was clear and cool that morning. The breeze brought them the salty tang of the sea and they could hear red-winged blackbirds calling in the scrub cedars that fringed the marsh.

There was nobody in sight when they reached the old Townsend property. They slipped into the brush, heading down toward the Sound. When they came to the edge of the clearing behind the log barn Andy motioned to his father to stay out of sight while he reconnoitered. As soon as he was sure the coast was clear they went on to the front of the little building. And there the boy came to a sudden stop.

"Gosh!" he whispered. "Look at that!"

The barn door had been pried from its hinges and hung askew, still held by the staple and padlock.

"Take it easy," said his father. "There's probably some tracks here, if we don't spoil 'em."

They went forward cautiously till they could see inside the barn. It had no windows but enough daylight entered through the wrecked door to show them it was empty. Only a few wisps of marsh hay lay scattered on the puncheon floor.

"Wonder who did it," Andy's father said with a frown. "Not Gillen, that's sure."

"I could make a pretty fair guess," the boy replied.

"Gowdy an' his friend, Stumpy, must have known about this place, an' they've been trying to get money out o' Gillen. I reckon they had a hand in it. Say—you said something about tracks—look there!"

In the sandy clay near the door there were footprints, blurred and confused. Andy knelt down to study them more closely, and his father joined him. Though the ground had been trampled it was possible to make out two different-sized tracks in the maze of prints. Two men had been there, one with a bigger foot than the other. And there was one rounded dent that might have been left by the end of a peg leg.

"These were made when it was muddy," Jeremiah Corson commented. "Last rain we had was the night you an' I were on our way to Philadelphia. So I figure they came here then or the next day. They must have known Gillen wouldn't be 'round for a while."

"When do you reckon he'll get back?" Andy asked.

"Depends on where he spent last night. If he stopped at May's Landing he won't get here till evening. But he's got a good team. Might ha' come all the way to Tuckahoe. In that case he'll make it before noon."

They followed the cart track down to the edge of the marsh and Andy showed his father how it led directly to Gillen's landing, at the head of Stites Sound.

They could see the garvey tied up there, and the Negro, Jim, doing something to the sail, spread out on the dock.

"Do you think Jim's in this with Gillen?" Andy asked, as they made their way back through the huckleberry thickets.

"I doubt if he realizes what they're doing," his father replied. "Jim's never had any schooling. He was a slave up to a few years ago, an' all he knows, now he's free, is to do what the boss tells him. He's strong, an' a good worker, an' I think he's honest."

It was some time after ten o'clock when they came out of the brush at the main road. They were out in the open and in plain sight when a creak of wheels caused Andy to look northward. There, just swinging into the lane that led to Gillen's farm, was a Jersey wagon pulled by a team that was all too familiar to him—a bay and a white-stockinged black. The distance was three or four hundred yards, but they could see Gillen's face turned in their direction as he stood in the front of the wagon.

"Well," said Jeremiah Corson grimly, "looks like he saw us, all right. He must ha' got a mighty early start this morning to be here now."

They talked very little on the way home, but Andy could sense a kind of tension in his father. He was apprehensive himself, for he couldn't escape the feeling that their chance encounter with Gillen might have the seeds of danger in it.

* * *

It was midafternoon when Andy came in from the south field. His father had sent him back to the barn for a grub hoe to dig out some old roots. As he passed the fish hawks' nest, he saw the mother osprey winging in from the sea. There was a foot-long fish in her talons, and as she settled on the rim of the nest he could see the heads of the young birds and their hungry, wide-open beaks. They were more than half grown now, and covered with fuzzy feathers.

As he watched them he heard a clatter of hoofs on the gravel of the dooryard. He hurried around the barn in time to see a big bay horse, sweating and foam-flecked, pulled to a stop. The rider was Beasley Gillen. He carried a shotgun across the pommel of his saddle, and his face was an ugly beet red.

"Where's Corson?" he roared, brandishing the gun.

"He—he's down in the field," Andy stammered.

"Well, get him up here," snarled the farmer. "An' make it quick."

Andy's fright had left him now. He was full of a cold, hard anger, and he stood his ground.

"Nobody orders my dad around that way," he retorted. "Nor me, either."

For a moment he thought the red-faced man would burst. Then Gillen answered, his voice choked with rage. "Listen, you sneakin' rat," he said. "I ought to shoot you down right here, but I'll wait till I catch you on my property again. You an' your ol' man both. I'll fill you so full o' buckshot you'll learn not to break into my buildin's! I own the Townsend place now, an' don't you forget it."

With that he jerked the horse's head around and went out of the yard at a wild gallop. Andy waited till he saw him start up the road, then got the grub hoe and ran all the way out to the south field.

"Dad!" he panted, as he came up. "Gillen was at the house. Had a gun with him an' told me to get you. I wouldn't do it, so he sent word he'd kill us if we ever went on his property again!"

Jeremiah Corson squared his shoulders. "*His* property?" he answered with a frown. "What's he talking about?"

"I don't know—but he says he owns the Townsend place now."

His father looked thoughtful as he rubbed his chin. "All right," he said finally, "you boys stay here an' get those roots out. I'm going down to the courthouse an' find out about this."

It was nearly suppertime when he returned. Andy and his brothers had done the evening chores and were in the kitchen, washing up. Mrs. Corson and the girls were putting the meal on the table.

"Well," said the farmer, "I had a talk with the sheriff an' the county clerk. Part o' what Gillen says is true. He bought the lower end o' the property last week—the part where the log barn stands. Paid hard cash for it, too."

Mrs. Corson stood with a dish of grape jelly in her hands. "What's this all about, Jeremiah?" she asked anxiously. "I saw that man outside an' heard him shouting at Andy. He sounded pretty angry about something."

"I might as well tell you the whole business," her husband answered. "Sit down an' we'll talk it over while we eat."

Methodically he gave them the story from the beginning. Once or twice he asked Andy to take over the narrative. The boy told of having found the locked barn and the scrap of red silk. He brought Becky into it then, to confirm the conversation they had overheard between Dode Gowdy and the lame man.

"That's what they said," she agreed eagerly. "An' I saw 'em both again Monday, when you an' Dad were gone to the city."

"The day it rained?" asked Andy.

"Yes, it was pouring. They came past just before

dark, walking toward the village, an' they were awfully wet. Ooh—how they were talking! Curses an' everything!"

"You shouldn't have listened," said her mother sternly.

"Well," Becky replied, "I didn't hear much—just that Stumpy was mad about something. He was the one that was swearing the most."

Andy looked at his father, who nodded. "It must have been that pair that broke into the barn," he said. "We found some foot tracks there, an' they'd been made when it was muddy."

Luke spoke up. "Gillen's a rough customer when anybody crosses him," he said. "What are we going to do—let him scare us?"

He met his father's steady glance and had no more to say.

Jeremiah Corson finished eating and pushed back his chair. "I talked to Sheriff Leaming," he told them. "He's had some suspicions of his own. I reckon there won't be any shooting—not by Gillen, anyhow."

That was Saturday night. The next morning, as Andy was putting on his new suit to wear to church, big Jess passed his door, still in his working clothes.

"You'd better hustle," Andy told him. "We ought to start in ten minutes."

"Guess I'll stay away from church today," his older brother told him with a grin.

This was something unbelievable. Andy stared open-mouthed. "You mean you're sick?" he asked.

"No, no," Jess laughed. "Dad figures maybe some-body'd better stay here. If Beasley Gillen thinks we broke into his old barn, he might decide Sunday morning was a good time to get even."

The rest of the family drove out of the yard and left Jess sitting comfortably on the front doorstep with Shep to keep him company. It was a fine summer day, and the congregation was a big one. But neither Mrs. Gillen nor Prudence Mayhew put in an appearance. Luke kept looking around at the pew where Prue usually sat, and his face grew longer and longer.

When the service was over Andy joined his brother in the churchyard. "Looks like you won't see her today," he said sympathetically.

"That's the trouble with these family fights," Luke replied. "They hurt the people that don't deserve it."

The other neighborhood boys came up then—Ned Swain, Joe Hand and Josh Ludlam. They were eager to hear about Andy's trip to Philadelphia, and for the next ten minutes he was the center of attention. Finally his father had to break up the gathering to get his family into the wagon.

When they got home Jesse came walking out from the barn to meet them.

"Any trouble?" asked his father.

"Not a bit," the big lad answered. "Gillen came riding past here about an hour ago, an' saw me loafing in the yard. He kept going. After a while he came back up the road. He was on that black horse with the white legs."

"Hmm," Jeremiah Corson grunted. "Guess it was just as well you stayed home. Soon as we've had dinner I think I'll go over to Dennis Creek an' try to get hold o' the revenue skipper."

He set off about two and was home before sundown. At the supper table he told them about his talk with Lieutenant Craig.

"The cutter was tied up in the creek, all right," he said. "There's a pair of 'em an' they take turns on patrol off the Capes. Craig says if he isn't there the other one will be. Naturally, what he's after is the smugglers' ships, but he's interested in the land end o' the business, too. Anything more we see or hear, he'd like to know about it. Funny thing—one o' the first questions he asked about Gillen was whether there was a fish hawk's nest on his place! I couldn't answer that one."

"There isn't any," Luke put in. "Prue says Mrs. Gillen doesn't like 'em."

Andy started to speak but decided to keep his idea to himself. He remembered the long-legged, drawling stranger on the bony nag, and his queer curiosity about fish hawks' nests. Now he began to think he knew who the man was.

CHAPTER XI

Two days later Jeremiah Corson suggested another trip to the island. It was a hot morning, and the light southerly breeze had a sultry feel to it. At breakfast the farmer commented that there wasn't much work that needed doing that day.

"I've been wondering," he said, "how the cattle are getting along. Might be a good idea for a couple of you to go over an' see. What about it, Luke? You an' Andy want to go?"

Andy had more enthusiasm for the trip than his brother, but Luke agreed without much urging. They got some fishing tackle together, packed a parcel of bread and meat and set out for the landing with Shep trotting ahead.

The tide was on the ebb but they dragged the skiff down to the water and launched it. There wasn't enough wind to use the sail. Two hours of steady pulling at the oars took them down through the winding channel that threaded Great Sound, and by ten-thirty they hauled the boat out on the flats near the same spot where Andy had landed earlier in the summer.

"Not much use trying to fish now, with the tide out," Andy remarked. "Let's go over to the beach an' have a swim. Maybe we'll see the cattle on the way."

They left their lunch in the boat and crossed through the woods to the dunes. There were cow tracks around the fresh-water pond but no cattle were in sight. There was a drowsy stillness over the island. The only thing that stirred was a tall blue heron, stalking frogs in the reeds at the edge of the pool. He looked them over with a cold and fearless eye but made no move to fly away.

The beach lay wide and white under the August sun. The boys stripped off their clothes and raced down the sand into the tumbling surf. For half an hour they swam and dove through the low breakers or rode them in. The water was just cold enough to make their skin tingle pleasantly, and when they came out the sun felt good on their tanned bare bodies.

"Some day," said Andy, "I suppose folks will come down from the city an' camp out here in the summer, just to swim an' keep cool. Maybe there'll even be a hotel, like they have at Cape Island."

"Ha!" Luke laughed scornfully. "Who'd come to a backwoods place like this? An' how'd they get here? There's no decent harbor for a steamboat, an' no road across the marsh or the sound. I reckon they'll still be pasturing cattle here a hundred years from now."

"An' smuggling!" Andy suggested with a chuckle. "Come on, let's walk up the beach."

Luke yawned and stretched his arms. "You go ahead," he said. "I'm going to take a nap up here in the shade of a dune. That swim made me sleepy."

Andy took the old collie with him for company and set off along the firm sand. He carried his shirt and jeans in his hand and as soon as the sun had dried him he put them on. The shore line looked unchanged since his last visit. Yet he knew it was always changing. The pieces of driftwood that had served for landmarks earlier in the season were gone now and new ones had taken their places. Once he came on the splintered end of a great spar nearly two feet in diameter. There was an iron band around it, and the frayed remnants of a tarred rope. He thought it might have been the topmast of a clipper, blown away in some gale that had swept the distant seas months before.

There were more birds on the beach now, he noticed. Great flocks of sandpipers scurried along at the edge of the ripples, pecking at the tiny purple shellfish that lay awash there. Two or three kinds of gulls sunned themselves on the sand or floated on the waves offshore. And graceful white terns skimmed above the breakers, darting down after the minnows that swam in the shoal water.

The boy and the dog had covered two miles or more when Andy recognized the spot where he had found the slaughtered heifer. All traces were gone now, swallowed by the smooth, shifting beach. But he could see the hollow at the foot of the dune where the killers had roasted their meat. Evidently they had not returned here, for even the charred logs were washed away or buried under the sand.

Andy headed north again, toward Townsend's Inlet and the upper end of the island. He had gone only a short distance when he saw a fish hawk coming shoreward. The big bird was only a hundred feet above the ocean, flying with slow, steady wing-beats. As it came nearer Andy could see that it was carrying a large fish, and he stood still to watch as he had done many times before. He always marveled at the way the osprey handled its awkward load. Gripped in those powerful claws, the still-struggling mackerel was held close to the bird's body, head forward and tail to the rear, offering the least possible resistance to the wind.

The boy waited, expecting the fish hawk to gain altitude and fly above the dunes toward the distant mainland. Instead, he was surprised to see the great wings stop beating and set for a downward glide. The bird sailed straight for the high dune. And when Andy looked in that direction he saw its intended landing place—a nest of sticks in the fork of a gnarled old cedar. The tree was taller than most of the other growth on the dune, and from where Andy stood it bore an odd resemblance to a cross. A stumpy gray arm stood out on either side near the top. It was in the crotch of one of these dead limbs that the nest had been built.

Shep gave his master an impatient look and started off up the beach. But Andy wasn't ready to go on. He had a queer feeling about that cross-shaped tree. It was as if he had seen it somewhere before and it ought to mean something to him. After a moment's hesitation he went to the foot of the dune and started to climb, his feet slipping in the loose sand. When he reached the top he found himself in a thicket of bayberry and cedar that discouraged any further advance. But he could see the tree with the nest only fifty yards away. He put up his arms to protect his face and pushed forward through the brush. To his surprise the thicket ended a short distance from the base of the old cedar. He came out into a small cleared space.

Andy's heart began to beat faster as he looked about him. The brush had been cut with an ax, and though no footprints were visible, the sand around the foot of the tree had a trampled appearance. Above his head, the mother fish hawk was feeding the young birds in the nest. She seemed disturbed by his approach. While he watched she rose with a heavy flapping of wings and circled high above the tree, looking downward anxiously.

The boy stepped closer to the tree. There was a hollowed-out place in the sand under one of the gray old roots, and tucked snugly into the hiding place was a rusty metal object. With mounting excitement he pulled it out. It was an old bull's-eye lantern, made to burn whale oil. He put it back where he had found it and stood up, looking more closely at the trunk of the tree. About five feet from the ground there was a big iron spike driven into the wood. And as he stared at it he made the most startling discovery of all. A straight, narrow opening had been cut through the underbrush beyond!

Andy bent his head till it was just below the spike.

Looking westward through the gap in the thicket he could see the waters of Stites Sound, the marsh at its farther edge and the fields of a farm above. Centered in his line of vision were a tiny house and barn that had a familiar look, even though they must have been three or four miles away. He knew then that he was looking at the buildings on Beasley Gillen's place.

Shep had come back and followed him up the dune. The old dog must have caught some of Andy's excitement, for he raced ahead as the boy hurried down to the beach. Together they ran southward.

"Go get Luke," Andy panted. "Wake him up an' bring him back with you." The collie seemed to understand the order. He loped off along the beach at a pace far faster than the boy could follow.

After a while Andy stopped running and sat down on the sand to wait. He could barely see Shep, a moving dot in the shimmering haze that lay over the beach. Minutes passed, and then there were two dots in the distance. They grew slowly larger and more distinct. The old dog had carried out his mission.

The boy got up and started down the beach to meet them. Luke was out of breath and had a worried look when he came up.

"What's the trouble?" he asked. "You hurt or something?"

Andy grinned. "No," he said, "I'm fine. I just

thought you'd been dozing long enough. Got something to show you."

"Humph!" Luke sounded disgruntled. "A dirty trick, I call it. The way Shep acted I figured at least you'd broken a leg. What's this you've found? I'm telling you right now it better be good!"

Andy pointed up the shore. "See that big old cedar on the top of the dune?" he said. "That's where we're going."

As they drew nearer Luke eyed the tree suspiciously. "Don't tell me you got me way up here just to look at a fish hawk's nest," he growled.

"This is sort of a special one," the younger boy replied. "I've got an idea it's the one that stranger was looking for—the fellow who talked like a Southerner. Come on an' see for yourself."

He led the way up the dune and through the brush. When they reached the foot of the tree he pulled the lantern out from under the root and hung it on the spike, its bull's-eye opening turned toward the mainland.

"All right," he said, "what do you make of that?"

Luke squinted past the lantern and whistled in surprise. "Gosh!" he exclaimed. "That's Gillen's farm—an' the landing. I can see his garvey tied up at the dock!"

"Now," said Andy, "suppose it was nighttime instead of daylight. If you lighted this lantern do you reckon Gillen could see it from the house?"

"Sure! An' that's the only place it would be in sight. The way the bushes are trimmed out, nobody could see the light from the main road."

Andy nodded. "You've got the idea," he said. "It would make a good signal light for somebody who wanted to let old Gillen know he was here, an' didn't want anybody else to find it out."

"Smugglers!" Luke whispered the word in his excitement. "Boy, we've got him dead to rights now!"

"There's just one thing more," said Andy. "How far would you say it was from here to Townsend's Inlet?"

"I don't know. Less'n half a mile I'd guess."

"I'm going to step it off," Andy replied. "An' I'll bet you a red apple it's just seven hundred paces."

His brother was mystified. "How would you know?" he asked.

"Just a hunch. I'll show you when we get home."

Andy started toward the beach, then stopped suddenly. To his left he saw a kind of path through the brush that he had not noticed before. It was barely wide enough for a man's body, but it led straight northward along the crest of the dune. Without hesitating he set off along the path, taking long strides and counting as he went.

Luke put the lantern back in its hole and followed

him, while Shep ranged alongside through the thicket. When Andy had reached six hundred in his count, the cedar growth thinned out and the ground dropped away sharply. There, right in front of them, hardly more than a stone's throw away, was the turbulent blue water of the inlet!

"Golly!" said Luke in wonder. "You hit it right on the nose. Another hundred steps an' you'd get your feet wet."

Andy nodded. "I was pretty sure," he replied. "An' this path proves it. Let's get those cattle counted an' head back. Come on, Shep. Go find the cows."

The old dog wagged his tail and started off at a purposeful trot. He had scented the herd long before and knew just where to locate them. Twenty minutes later the boys, hurrying in his wake, heard his deep bark from the woods ahead.

Shep had the cows and calves rounded up in a grassy savanna near the middle of the island. The boys came quietly out of the woods and saw them switching flies and chewing their cuds. They showed none of the nervous wildness that Andy had found in the herd on his previous trip.

"You count an' I will, too," whispered Luke.

They moved slowly around the edge of the meadow till they had been able to see all the cows, calves and yearlings.

"I make it fifty-two," Andy murmured. "What's your count?"

"The same—just fifty-two. Must be some new calves since you were over here."

"That's right," said Andy. "An' all the rest are on hand, so we know there hasn't been any more killing. Come on—let's go fishing. The tide's turned an' they ought to be hungry. Anyhow, I know I am."

It was an hour past noon when they got back to the boat. The tide was running strongly up-channel now, and they anchored near a marshy bend, dropped their baited hooks over and attacked the lunch they had brought from home. Andy had eaten only a mouthful or two when he felt a tug on his line. He hauled in gently, uncertain whether he had a real bite.

"Feels like a crab," he remarked. "No fight—just a pull. Here, let me have that crab net."

But while the hook was still a fathom down he could see a flat, silvery shape twirling at the end of the line. "Fluke!" he exclaimed. "Boy—a nice one! Ought to run two pounds!"

"I got one, too," Luke announced as he pulled in line. "We must be over a nest of 'em."

They landed five good-sized flounder almost as fast as they could bait up and get their lines in the water. Then the flurry ended abruptly. They finished their lunch, moved to another spot and then another, but the bottom-fish were no longer biting. In the next two hours all they caught were a croaker and a small weakfish.

Luke yawned. "How about starting back?" he said. "If we want these fluke for supper we'd better get 'em home to Mom. I know you'd fish all night, but I get tired of it when they won't bite. Besides, you promised to show me something—remember?"

CHAPTER XII

BY THE TIME the boys had reached home, cleaned the catch and turned the fish over to their mother, it was after five o'clock. The evening chores had to be done. So Andy had no opportunity to show Luke his secret until after supper.

In the barn he pulled the mahogany box from its hiding place behind the grain bin, blew off the dust and opened it.

"I found it buried in the sand on the beach," he explained. "That was back in June, the time the heifer was killed. It had just two things in it—the Spanish dollar an' this piece o' wood. See the words cut on it? I never could figure out what it was all about until today."

He held out the little carved slab for Luke's inspection. " 'Signel' seemed clear enough, even if it was spelled wrong, an' I thought 'T. Inlet' must stand for Townsend's Inlet. That cross-shaped jigger looked like a tree with a bird flying over it. But the 'S. 700' didn't mean anything special. It wasn't till I found the fish hawk's nest an' the lantern this morning that the whole thing began to make sense. Now you know why I was so sure it would be seven hundred paces south from the shore o' the inlet."

Luke nodded eagerly. "I get it," he said. "An' o' course the last line means 'wait one tide.' That's to give Gillen enough water to bring his garvey out across the Sound. But who do you think cut the words? An' why?"

"Well," said Andy, "suppose this smuggling's been going on for years. Different ships an' different skippers come in to unload their cargo. A strange one would have to have directions to find the signal tree an' let Gillen know they were there. Remember that schooner that was wrecked winter before last? I reckon this box might have come from her captain's cabin. Maybe some other smuggler gave him the piece o' wood with the directions on it, an' he put it away for safekeeping. The box was locked tight, so it would float all right, an' it probably got washed ashore after the wreck."

"Sounds reasonable," Luke replied thoughtfully. "Gosh—imagine old Gillen being in the business so long an' nobody suspecting! What's the next thing to do, now we know how they work?"

"Catch 'em at it, if we can. Any night now there might be a ship coming in. Can you get word to Prudence somehow—so she could let us know if she sees the lantern lighted?"

" 'Twon't be easy," said Luke, "but I'll try. I know she'll help all she can. Because if Gillen gets caught smuggling an' sent to jail, maybe she won't have to serve out the rest of her indenture time! Reckon I'll go over an' try to see her tonight."

He set off up the road in the deepening dusk, and Andy returned to the house. About nine o'clock, when Becky had been sent off to bed and the elder Corsons were about to go upstairs, Jesse came in. He was red-faced and out of breath from hurrying.

"Heard some news," he panted. "Down in the village. Dode Gowdy was in the store, talking to Enoch Hughes. Says his friend Stumpy's disappeared. Don't know why anybody'd worry about a no-'count clam-digger like him, but Gowdy was really upset. He's sure something's happened to him. Wants the sheriff to get up a posse an' search the woods an' the marsh."

Jeremiah Corson smiled. "I expect folks are laughing at him," he commented. "The shiftless critter's probably sleeping off a bout with the bottle."

"Well," Jess replied, "there were some people in the store that took it as a joke. But not Hughes. He acted 'most as upset as Gowdy. He's not a man to scare easy, but he got sort o' white when he heard about it. Anyhow, Dode has dug up four or five men from 'round the village an' they're aiming to start a hunt as soon as it's daylight."

Andy had been listening with close attention. Remembering the threat Stumpy had made to get something out of Gillen, he was inclined to agree with Gowdy's idea. However, he kept his mouth shut and shortly went upstairs to bed. For an hour or more he lay there, unable to get to sleep. Then he heard a floor board creak outside his door. He sprang out of bed and tiptoed across the room.

"Hey, Luke!" he whispered. "Is that you?"

"Sh!" his brother answered. "I thought everybody

was asleep." He slipped in and closed the door silently behind him.

"Did you get to talk to Prue?" Andy asked.

"Yes. She's found a way to get out—by the big maple tree that grows outside her window. I tossed some gravel at the glass an' she came down. Prue says she'll keep watch for a light on the dune, an' if she sees it, she's promised to run over here an' tell us. Poor kid—she's really scared now."

"Why—has something new happened?"

Luke hesitated. "I don't know. Anyhow, she thinks so. There was some sort of commotion out around the barn last night. The chickens were squawking, an' Gillen took his gun an' went out. After a few minutes she heard the gun go off. Then she says it was a long time—maybe an hour—before Gillen came back. I told her it was probably just a fox or a 'coon after the hens, but she doesn't think so. Prue says the old man acted so strange this morning she hardly dared open her mouth for fear he'd beat her."

"Strange?" asked Andy. "How do you mean he acted strange?"

"All I know is what she told me. He's always crusty an' hard-tempered, but this morning he was jumpy, besides. Kept looking out the window an' listening for something."

Andy told him the news about the clam-digger's

mysterious disappearance. "Had they heard anything about it at Gillen's?" he asked. "Prue didn't mention seeing Stumpy around there, did she?"

"No," said Luke. "Not many folks ever go near their place. Well, it's getting late. I'm going to bed."

It was cloudy next morning, and by noon a steady rain was falling. Since it was impossible to do any field work in that kind of weather, Jeremiah Corson set the boys to doing odd jobs indoors. Luke whittled out new rungs for the ladder that led up to the hayloft while Jess and Andy repaired a broken wagon tire. There was a small forge in the shed that adjoined the barn. Jess, who was a pretty fair blacksmith, handled the tongs and the hammer, and Andy fed the fire and worked the bellows.

They heated the broken ends of the iron hoop, welded in a new piece and brought the whole tire to a dull cherry red. Meanwhile Andy had filled an old horse trough with water. When the hot tire had been hammered onto the wooden rim of the wheel, they plunged it, sizzling and smoking, into the trough and turned it till the cold water had shrunk the iron tight to the wood.

They were greasing the axle before putting the wheel back on the wagon when Amos Diverty, one of their neighbors from up the road, came into the yard. He had just come from the village, and he got off his horse to dry out for a moment and pass the time of day.

"How's the great man hunt coming along?" Jess asked him with mock seriousness.

Diverty grinned. "They all gave up soon as the rain got heavy," he replied. "Even Dode Gowdy was ready to quit after five or six hours o' trampin' around. I guess now most folks think Stumpy must ha' got hold o' some money somewhere an' lit out for a spree. Maybe up to May's Landing or Green Bank. Anyhow, I doubt if anybody's likely to care how long he stays away."

He remounted and rode off. Jess was still chuckling over the account of the search party, but Andy wasn't sure it was funny. He had a feeling that the one-legged man might have done something rash and put himself in real danger.

The long day of rain ended at last, and by next morning the skies had cleared. At breakfast they were discussing the work that needed doing. Jeremiah Corson remarked that the ground was still too wet to accomplish anything worth-while in the fields. And the words were hardly out of his mouth when Becky spoke up.

"Dad," she said, "you promised to let Andy take me fishing some time. Why wouldn't this be a good day for it?"

"I don't know," said her father. "Maybe your ma needs you around the house."

"No, no," Mrs. Corson replied. "Far's I'm concerned she can go, if you can spare Andy."

That settled it. As soon as Becky had washed the dishes she told her brother she was ready to start. Andy accepted the plan with good grace. He wasn't too happy to have a girl tagging along, but he would never pass up a chance to fish. At least he didn't have to prepare the lunch. Becky took care of that while he got together two sets of tackle.

His sister chatted amiably on the way down to the landing and helped him dig some clams for bait. They launched the skiff and sailed out across the Sound with a light southerly breeze abeam. Andy dropped anchor at a likely spot near a bend in the channel.

They had been fishing for perhaps ten minutes when Becky surprised her brother with a question.

"You think Stumpy's dead, don't you?" she asked out of a clear sky.

"Why?" he returned defensively.

"Because you an' I know he was trying to get even with Gillen an' make him pay over some money. Anybody that's a smuggler wouldn't be afraid to kill a man who made trouble for him, would he?"

"Maybe not," said Andy. "But after all, smuggling's one thing an' murder's another."

"Both things are wicked," the girl replied firmly. "Besides, Gillen looks mean enough to kill a man."

Her brother decided to change the subject. "Remember that little piece of carved wood in the box I found on the beach?" he asked. "Well, you were right about that thing that looked like a cross. You said it was meant to be a tree with a bird flying over it, an' that's just what it is—a big cedar an' a fish hawk's nest in the top. Luke an' I found it, over on the dune."

"Does it have something to do with smuggling?" she asked breathlessly.

Andy nodded. "Looks like it. There's a bull's-eye lantern there that can be hung on the tree for a signal."

"Gracious sakes!" the girl exclaimed. "Then if we watch for it an' see the light, that means there's smugglers on the island!"

"No," he replied. "Because it can't be seen except from one place—Beasley Gillen's farm."

Their talk was interrupted by a sharp tug on Becky's line, and for the next half hour there was plenty of action. When it was over they had pulled in four small sea bass and two weakfish.

They waited for some time after that without getting a nibble. Andy pulled up the anchor and rowed a mile down the channel to another good fishing hole he knew. There they added two good-sized flounder to the catch before noon.

"Let's go ashore on the island," Becky suggested.

"It'll be cooler there under the trees, an' we can find some fresh water to drink when we eat lunch."

They were not far from Andy's usual landing place. He rowed the boat across and they walked up through the marsh grass to the woods. Sitting beside the little pool they ate the food Becky had brought.

The breeze had died down during the morning and the air was heavy and still. When they came out from under the trees, Andy looked over to the west and urged his sister to hurry.

"Look at that cloud bank," he said. "There'll be thundersqualls this afternoon, an' if we don't hustle we'll get caught in 'em."

He shoved off in haste. The dark curtain in the west crept up the sky and before he had rowed a mile against the tide, the cloud's edge had covered the sun. In the distance they could hear a low, steady growl of thunder.

Luckily, when the wind came it was from the south. Andy stepped the mast as quickly as he could and spread the sail. The skiff heeled over, rushing through the water.

"Hang on!" the boy shouted. "Hook your feet under the thwart an' lean back over the side!"

He held the steering oar with one hand and threw his weight to port, clinging to the straining sheet. It took skillful sailing to bring the boat across the Sound in those gusts of wind, but they made it without capsizing.

The first big drops of rain were beginning to fall when they came up to the landing. Andy ran in full tilt and beached the skiff on the mud-flat before taking in sail.

"Get going!" he yelled over his shoulder at Becky. "You'll have to run or you'll be mighty wet! I'll bring the fish."

But when he had stowed the mast and pulled the boat up beyond the tide line he discovered his sister still standing by the edge of the water.

"Come here," she said, in a choked voice.

He picked up the fish and hurried to her side while the rain came down harder and harder. She was pointing at something that floated among the reeds, a dozen yards out from shore. It was a dark, shapeless thing, lying almost submerged, and it rose and fell sluggishly with the waves.

"What is it?" he cried, through the growing tumult of the rain.

"A man!" she answered. "I—I saw the face!"

As he watched, the thing turned slowly and a pale oval appeared, half under water. With a sick feeling, Andy dropped the string of fish and plunged in. The water by the reeds was only up to his waist. He reached the floating object in a few strides and stood horrified as an eddy of the tide swung it against him. An arm slithered along his thigh and the face was turned upward to the drenching rain.

Andy shuddered. If he had not recognized the slack mouth and staring, lifeless eyes, the wooden leg trailing in the water would have told him it was Stumpy. Quickly he seized the body under the shoulders and dragged it to shore.

"You'd better get up to the house," he told Becky roughly. "This is nothing for girls to look at."

She set off at a run through the downpour. When she was gone, Andy pulled the waterlogged corpse out on the marsh and turned it over. The back, under the ragged shirt, was one huge, gaping gunshot wound.

CHAPTER XIII

THE NEWS SPREAD FAST through Middle Township. By the time Andy reached home, Becky had told the family about finding the body, and Luke had ridden off to the village. Within half an hour a score or more of citizens gathered at the Corsons' landing, braving the rain that still fell.

Sheriff Leaming was among the first to arrive. He was a big, paunchy man with a walrus mustache, easy-going in most things but firm when it came to matters of the law. With him was the local physician, Dr. Way.

"Seemed like we ought to have a medical opinion," the sheriff told Jeremiah Corson. "So I brung the doc along. We better get along down an' view the remains."

Andy led the little procession to the landing. The doctor, a wiry, gray-whiskered little man, always overworked, knelt beside the body and gave it a quick examination.

"How long would ye say he'd been dead, Doc?" Leaming asked.

"Can't tell exactly but I'd estimate at least twenty-four hours," the doctor replied. "No signs o' drowning. He was dead when he went into the water."

He probed into the raw flesh of the back and pulled out a lead pellet that was bigger than a pea. "Buckshot," he commented briefly. "Caught the whole charge in the heart an' lungs. It cut the spinal cord, too. He couldn't have lived more'n a minute after he was hit."

The sheriff stooped over and spanned the wound with his big hand. " 'Bout ten inches across," he commented. "Shot hadn't scattered much. I'd say the gun was fired from fifty or sixty feet, dependin' on the choke. What do you think, Corson?"

"That's about right," Andy's father replied. "We could try it, firing at a board, if you want."

"Don't believe it's necessary," said Leaming. "We all know shotguns, an' we can guess close enough. The thing we've got to find out is who fired the gun. Anybody know whether Stumpy had any enemies?"

There was general silence among the onlookers.

Finally one of the villagers found words. "He was sort of a worthless cuss," he said, "but shucks—I can't imagine anybody wantin' to shoot him!"

The others nodded agreement.

"All right," Leaming went on, "let's see if it could ha' been an accident. I'd say no. Never heard of a feller shootin' himself in the middle o' the back. Besides, far's I know he didn't own a gun.

"So," he continued, "there's just one way to figger it. Somebody must have took him for an animal or a prowler an' shot at him in the dark. Only, if that was the way of it, how did his body get in the Sound? An' the answer is, it was put there by the man that killed him. I guess I'll have to go to work."

They brought a light wagon down to the shore and bundled the body into it, wrapped in a tarpaulin.

"Stumpy didn't have any kinfolk that we know of," the sheriff remarked. "An' he didn't belong to any church. So he'll have to be buried in public ground. I reckon the place to put him is in that lot back o' the courthouse where Zeke Jenkins used to pasture his mule. There's other paupers buried there. Old Injun Charlie for one—the poor old sot that claimed he was King Nummy's son."

Before the afternoon was over, Leaming was going methodically from house to house, talking to every man in the community whose property was within a mile of the Sound. He made such a call at the Corsons'. First he asked to see any firearms on the place and inquired when they had last been used. Then he asked bluntly if Jeremiah or one of his boys had killed the one-legged clam-digger. And the answer to each question was laboriously written down in a book he carried.

It took the sheriff two days to complete his rounds of the farms. Before he had finished, the mortal remains of Stumpy had been put in a plain cedar box and laid to rest in the weed-grown lot behind the county buildings. There were few actual mourners, but the crowd that assembled for the burial would have done credit to one of the township's leading citizens. One man, Dode Gowdy, was conspicuous by his absence. People talked about that. Some thought he was too deeply affected by his friend's death to appear in public. But there were others who hinted the clam-digger had a guilty conscience. They remembered that he had been seen, in years past, hunting ducks with an old fowling-piece.

Gradually the excitement that had followed the discovery of the body died down. Sheriff Leaming kept his own counsel and made no arrests. If he suspected anybody, it was impossible to guess it. The neighbors went back to their routine of work, but some of them bolted their doors at night—a thing that had been practically unheard-of in the county.

Knowing what he did, Andy was sorely tempted to give his information to the sheriff. But Luke argued against it.

"He's talked to the Gillens," he reminded his younger brother. "An' he probably asked Prudence some questions, too. If she didn't tell him anything, there was a good reason. Beasley'd beat her black an' blue. You just wait, Andy. I've got a hunch things'll be coming to a head 'most any day now."

The weather stayed hot all that week. They went about their farm work but kept an eye on the west, where thunderclouds occasionally gathered. But the storms sheered off, moving up the Delaware, and they had no rain for several days.

One sultry evening the rumbling sound of distant thunder was louder than usual. Jeremiah Corson sent the boys out to shut the doors of the barn and other buildings.

"Shouldn't wonder if this one might hit us," he told them. "Better be safe."

Andy was returning to the house in the early dark when he saw a red glow in the sky to the northeast. It was faint at first but it grew brighter as he watched. Racing to the door he called to his parents.

"There's a fire up the shore a way," he shouted. "Looks like Gillen's place."

His father came out at once. "Get some buckets together," he ordered. "You, Jess, hitch up to the wagon quick. We'll get over there as fast as we can."

They galloped up the road, clinging to the sides of the swaying wagon. There were other vehicles and riders before and behind them, for in case of a fire the whole community turned out. By the time they reached the lane leading to Gillen's buildings they could see flames towering above the trees, and the black figures of men scurrying like ants in front of the blazing barn.

Hitching the horses to a fence rail, they grabbed their buckets and ran to join the line that had formed at the well. It was obvious that nothing could be done to save the barn. Part of the roof was gone and the hay inside was like a roaring furnace. The bucket-line was putting all its energies into protecting the house and sheds from the showers of sparks.

As Andy worked, passing the slopping pails from hand to hand, he saw bewildered livestock wandering about the barnyard. Someone must have reached the scene in time to get the cattle and horses out. The big bay and the white-stockinged black were securely tied by their halters to the back of the Jersey wagon, but they reared and screamed and rolled their eyes in terror.

Beasley Gillen staggered back and forth in an aimless frenzy. His beard was singed and smoking, and his eyes had the wild, staring look of a madman. A steady stream of curses came from his twisted mouth.

In less than half an hour the barn lay in a smoldering ruin. By heroic work they had saved the other buildings, and now the rain began, accompanied by lightning and thunder. One by one the neighbors left the scene and hurried toward home. As the Corsons got into their wagon, Andy saw a hulking figure in the gloom beyond the fence. It was moving off in the direction of the woods but he was almost sure he recognized Dode Gowdy.

"Hey!" he said to his brothers. "Did you see that? The fellow heading for the woods. I thought it was Gowdy."

"Sure, he was in the bucket-line when we got there," Luke replied. "Must have been one o' the first. That's a queer thing, too. How'd he make it so fast if he was afoot?"

"Anybody hear how the fire started?" Jess asked.

His father shook the reins and clucked to the horses. "I heard some say 'twas a bolt of lightning," he said. "I don't believe it, though. That storm was too far off. Gillen was raving an' didn't make much sense, but I gather he thinks the fire was set."

"So do I," Luke put in unexpectedly. "Prue says she caught a glimpse of a man out back o' the barn, about ten minutes before they smelled the first smoke. The sheriff must think somebody set it, too, for he was back there looking around."

* * *

A burned barn is a disturbing thing in any farm neighborhood. For days the township buzzed with rumors that Sheriff Leaming was about to make an arrest. By that time it was the general belief that the fire had been started, either by mischievous boys or by some enemy of Gillen's. But still the jail stood empty.

Then someone noticed that Dode Gowdy hadn't been seen around his usual haunts since the night of the fire. The gossips put two and two together and concluded that he was the guilty man—an idea on which the sheriff refused to comment.

All he would say was, "If there's a firebug around, we're going to catch him sooner or later."

It was several days after that when Andy saw the lanky stranger on the livery nag for the second time. The man rode into the yard at eight o'clock one morning. Andy had just finished feeding the pigs and was ready to join his father and brothers in the south field.

"Mr. Corson anywhere about?" the stranger inquired.

"He's down there doing some hoeing," said the boy, pointing toward the field. "I'll show you the way."

The man swung a long leg over the cantle and dismounted with what sounded like a sigh of relief. "Sho' glad to get out o' that saddle for a spell," he said. "Horses aren't much in my line, I'm afraid."

They started across the oat stubble. "You're Lt. Craig, aren't you?" Andy asked.

"That's right. An' I reckon you must be the lad your father spoke of—the one who figured out how the smugglers work."

Andy was pleased. "I've found out some more," he said. "Over on the island—the place where they put their signal light."

"That so? What sort of a place?"

"It's a big old dead cedar with a fish hawk's nest in the top."

The revenue officer stopped in the middle of a stride, and Andy, looking back at him in surprise, saw his long jaw harden and his gray eyes gleam.

"So you've found it!" he said. "The fish hawk's nest—I've been looking for it for months!"

Andy stared at him. "But"—he faltered—"how did you know that was what you had to find?"

Craig had started walking again, hurrying his steps. "It's a long story, lad," he answered. "I'll tell it to you, but first I'd like a word with your father."

They found Jeremiah Corson, hoe in hand, in the lower field. When the greetings were over, the lieutenant came to the point at once.

"I want to borrow your son for a few hours," he said. "There are some things he's found over on Seven Mile Beach, and I need him for a guide."

Andy's father nodded. "I guess the boy knows the island about as well as anybody," he agreed. "An' the work isn't so pressing he can't be spared. Take him, an' welcome."

The youngster had to hustle to keep up with Craig on the way back. They stopped only a moment at the house, where the revenue man saw to the hitching of his horse and Andy ran to the barn. When he returned he had the little piece of wood in his pocket. They went directly to the landing then, and launched the boat. The tide was full and there was a spanking southwest breeze.

Once on the water a complete change came over the tall officer. No longer clumsy in his movements, he took the skiff out across the Sound like an oldtime bayman. With his legs stretched out and the wind ruffling his hair, he lay back on the stern thwart and handled the sheet so expertly that the skiff was fairly skimming over the water.

"I guess you've been in small boats before," said Andy with respect.

Craig grinned. "I grew up in 'em," he replied, "down on the Eastern Shore o' Maryland. I don't know your channel here but we seem to have enough water. Where do you want to land?"

The boy directed him to a good spot on the shore and he ran her in smartly. They beached the boat and set off at once across the island.

"Now," said the cutter commander, "I'll try to explain why I was so interested in fish hawks' nests. It started back in the spring. We were cruising off the mouth o' the Chesapeake, and one foggy morning we had the luck to come on a smuggling ship. She was schooner-rigged and fast, but we were within short cannon-range when we sighted each other through the fog. I ordered her to heave to and her skipper tried to run for it.

"Well, it wasn't much of a fight, as naval engagements go. Our first broadside cut some of her rigging and swept her quarterdeck, and the captain had had enough. After he struck his colors we boarded her and found the cargo we expected—smugglers' goods from France and the West Indies. So I put a prize crew aboard her and took her into Norfolk.

"Only one man had been hit by our shot—the first mate. His wound was pretty bad, so we put him in a berth in the cutter's cabin and had our surgeon look after him. That night he was delirious. At first the surgeon didn't pay much attention to what he was saying, but after a while he asked me to come below and listen. In his fever dreams the mate was giving orders to his crew. Between us we knew enough Spanish to understand some of what he said, and there was one thing he repeated over and over.

" 'When you get ashore,' he kept saying, 'you must find the fish hawk's nest. It will lead you to the man who will pay for the cargo.' That didn't make much sense to me, but after I'd heard it a dozen times I couldn't forget it.

"When the fellow got better I put him through a lot of questioning. He wouldn't admit ever hearing of such a thing as a fish hawk's nest, but he did let it slip that the schooner had been heading for some part o' the Jersey Coast. So in June, when I was ordered to the Cape May station, I started looking for nests along the shore road."

He paused, chuckling to himself. "Never saw so many fish hawks' nests in my life!" he said. "There was one in nearly every farmyard. They just about drove me crazy. But if you've located the right one it's worth all the trouble."

CHAPTER XIV

WHILE CRAIG HAD BEEN TALKING they had crossed the island and descended the dune. Now they were moving northward along the beach at the same rapid pace. Andy took the carved chip from his pocket.

"Two months ago," he said, "I found this in the sand, up here at the edge o' the dunes. It was in a little wooden chest that looked as if it had washed ashore quite a while before. Can you read those letters cut on it?"

Craig's brow furrowed in concentration as he studied the bit of wood. Then his face cleared and he slapped his thigh. "I get it!" he exclaimed. "South seven hundred yards from the inlet—is that what it means?"

"Yes," said Andy, "an' that's just where the tree is, with a bull's-eye lantern all ready to hang."

"Come on, then," the revenue man urged. "We're wasting time."

They reached the ospreys' nest in half an hour of fast walking. The older birds were not in sight, but the fledglings squawked plaintively in their sprawling home of sticks at the top of the tree.

Andy got the lantern from the hole under the root and hung it in place on the spike. "Now," he said, "if you sight past it through that gap in the brush, you'll see a farm—Gillen's farm."

Craig looked, nodded and straightened up again. "That ties it up," he said crisply. "If we don't catch 'em now we'll be pretty stupid. I could arrest Gillen on this much evidence, but we'll have a solid case if we take him and the smugglers with the goods."

Andy explained the plan for Prudence to give them a warning whenever she saw the signal light.

"Then," he said, "one of us'll ride across to Dennis Creek an' let you know. We could get there in an hour."

The lieutenant scratched his chin and thought it over.

"There might be a quicker way," he said after a moment. "It's always possible both cutters may be out at once. What we need is a sure way to get the word to us. You know the high bluff, over on the bay shore above Cape Island?"

"Yes," said Andy. "It's only about ten miles from our place."

"Well, a good big fire on the top of the bluff could be seen clear across to the Delaware shore. If the *Valiant* happened to be cruising anywhere in the bay, we'd know what it meant. My idea is to have the crew build up a pile o' wood for a bonfire and have dry tinder handy, so it could be set off in a hurry. If the smugglers have to wait over a tide that gives us up to twelve hours—probably seven or eight at the least. And with any kind of breeze we ought to reach Townsend's Inlet before they can get away."

Andy's eyes were shining. "Gee!" he murmured. "I sure hope I can be here to see it!"

They left the place as they had found it, carefully brushing away such tracks as they had made in the sand of the dune top. On the way back, Craig was relaxed and talkative. He told the boy about some of his adventures in the revenue service, from the time, three years earlier, when he had left his Chesapeake fishing to sign on aboard a cutter.

"There's a deal more smuggling going on than most

folks would suspect," he said. "We manage to catch as many as a dozen ships in a month, but we know there are more than that getting through. There must be hundreds of fast schooners and brigs in the business. And a lot of rascals ashore are getting rich out of it, too. Your friend Gillen is just one of 'em."

At the fresh-water pool in the middle of the island they stopped to drink. Andy glanced at the cattle tracks in the mud of the bank and paused suddenly, stooping for a closer look. Among the hoofmarks was the print of a man's naked foot, made within the last few hours.

Craig examined it, too. "Looks like a pretty good-sized fellow," he commented. "Do many grown men go barefoot around here?"

"No," said Andy. "Only a few clam-diggers an' such—the kind o' folks we call marsh-rats."

He said no more at the time, but the word had made him think of Dode Gowdy. The woods and thickets of the sea islands would be a fine place for a hunted man to hide. Uneasily he looked around him through the trees, but only the birds stirred there.

They were back on the mainland by noon. Lt. Craig refused Mrs. Corson's hearty invitation to stay for dinner, but he had a few words with her husband before he rode away.

During the meal Andy told the family about their

morning on the island, and described Craig's plan for a warning fire on the bluffs of the bay shore.

"That's right," Jeremiah Corson nodded. "He told me this would change our first idea. Instead o' riding to Dennis Creek, we're to go straight over to the bluff, soon as we get the word. That's to take care o' the chance of unfavorable winds an' tides in the creek. Whichever cutter is on patrol will see the signal and make all sail around the Cape."

"When do you think the smugglers will come?" Becky asked in excitement.

Luke laughed at her. "Maybe tonight," he said, "an' maybe not for weeks or months. Don't hold your breath waiting for 'em."

The colt, Starlight, had been out to pasture for the past few days. That evening Andy brought him up to the barn, curried him and gave him grain. He intended to have the young horse ready for a fast ride whenever the time should come.

For twenty-four hours after the lieutenant's visit the whole Corson household was keyed up with expectancy. Then, as day after day went by without incident, they spent less time thinking about smugglers. The last week of August passed. Beans had to be harvested and shelled, and then it was time for digging potatoes. When the last bushel was in the cellar, Jeremiah Corson set the boys to picking apples.

"That'll keep you busy while your mother and I are away," he said. "Next week they're having camp meeting down at Cape Island, an' I've promised to take her. The girls'll cook your meals an' look after you."

They set off early on the following Tuesday morning, dressed in their best and in a holiday mood. The gray horse pulled the light wagon, and in a box behind the seat Mrs. Corson had packed enough food to supply a regiment.

"Good-bye, my dears," she called, waving gaily to the five young people. "Take care o' things. We'll be back Thursday."

Elvira waved her apron in return. "I'm so glad they're going," she said. "Mother hasn't had a real rest for a year. They'll see all their friends an' have a wonderful time."

The trees in the orchard were heavy with fruit—big, sound apples, red-cheeked and juicy. Andy found it a temptation to bite into every one he picked, but when he had eaten three or four he was ready to settle down to the job.

Luke was working on the other side of the tree. From his perch on the ladder he called across to Andy. "I saw Prue last night," he said.

"That so? How are things over at Gillens'?"

"Tougher'n ever for her. The old man's grouchy

as a bear with a sore paw. He hasn't even started to build a new barn. If it had happened to most folks they'd have invited the neighbors for a barn-raising, an' it'd have been up an' roofed by now. Not Gillen, though. He's so suspicious of everybody, these days, he wouldn't let a neighbor on the place."

By chore time that evening they had picked more than thirty bushels of apples and packed them in barrels for winter keeping in the cellar. The girls had prepared a good supper and they all sat around the table for a while after the meal was ended. Jess was the first to rise.

"Guess I'll go down to the village," he said, so casually that the others laughed. They knew he had a romantic interest in Faith Leaming, the sheriff's daughter.

When he had changed his clothes and gone whistling down the road, Luke and Andy helped their sisters with the dishes. The September dusk had fallen, and they finished the job by lamplight. The girls settled down with their knitting and sewing, and Andy found a book to read. Luke was restless.

After a few minutes he went out and they heard the kitchen door close. "Off to Gillens' again," Elvira sighed. "Well, Andy, I guess you'll have to be the man of the family."

But in less than half an hour they heard Luke come

back. The door slammed and hurried footsteps came through the kitchen. Then the boy stood in the circle of light and there was someone with him. It was Prudence Mayhew, gasping for breath, her face wet with tears.

"Why, Prue!" cried Elvira. "What's wrong?"

"Plenty," Luke answered for her. "There's a light on the dune! She doesn't know whether Gillen saw her leave or not, but she ran all the way. I met her up the road a piece."

Andy was on his feet, shaking with excitement. "She ought to stay here," he said. "You girls take care of her. We've got to work fast."

Luke nodded. "Gillen's going to be too busy to look for Prue," he said, "an' if the revenue men catch him I hope she'll never have to go back there."

"We've got to get that signal fire lighted," said Andy. "You know the way, Luke. I'll saddle Starlight for you while you get ready. Be sure you have flint an' steel."

He ran to the barn with a lantern, led the black colt from his stall and threw the saddle on his back. He had pulled the cinch tight and was buckling the throatlatch of the bridle when his brother came out.

"I'm all set," said Luke. "But Starlight's your colt. I thought you'd want to ride him. What are you planning to do?"

Andy tried to keep his voice steady. "Oh," he said, "I guess I'll go over to the island."

"What? Boy—you're hunting trouble, aren't you? Better be mighty careful to keep out o' sight!"

Luke vaulted into the saddle and Starlight was off in a flash of flying hoofs.

Andy stood there and watched them till the colt vanished in the darkness down the road. He knew better than to reveal his plan to the girls. They would only raise a fuss if they found out where he was going. He stole in by the back way, got his light shotgun and loaded it. Outside again, he whistled softly till Shep appeared.

"Come on, boy," he whispered. "We're going for a boat ride."

When they reached the landing the tide was nearly out. That meant he had to drag the skiff twenty yards over the mud-flats but, he reflected, it also meant Gillen would have been unable to take the garvey out. Another five or six hours were bound to pass before the clumsy bay-boat could navigate the Sound. There was practically no wind and the night was dark. Andy rowed cautiously, taking soundings with an oar from time to time to make sure he was following the channel. Twice he ran aground on the flats and had to get overboard to push off.

It must have taken him close to two hours to reach

the island. When he got there he pulled the boat as far up as he could and made the anchor fast in case the returning tide should float her.

Shep was eager to set off in search of the cows, but the boy sternly ordered him to heel. "You stay with me," he commanded. "Maybe I should have left you home. Anyhow, now you're here you've got to keep quiet."

Crossing the wooded island in black darkness was no easy job, Andy discovered. After blundering into several trees he was glad to let the dog guide him. As nearly as he could tell it was about midnight when they finally topped the dune and made the descent to the beach.

On the open sands it was easier to see where he was going. He had traveled northward less than half a mile when a red flicker of light appeared, far up the beach. It increased gradually in size, and as he drew nearer he could see tiny figures moving in front of it. The smugglers must have built a bonfire at the foot of the dune, probably in the same place they had done it before. The collie's hackles were up and he was growling deep in his throat.

Andy wound his fingers tightly into the dog's ruff and told him to keep quiet. They were still too far away for him to make out just what the men were doing, but he didn't dare come any closer. After watching for a moment, he took Shep up over the dune and felt his way north through the cedar growth. He had no particular idea in mind except that he wanted to be on the scene when the smuggling ship and her crew were captured.

Moving slowly among the trees, he had covered some distance when Shep warned him with another low growl. The darkness in front of him seemed to be less intense, and after a few more steps he realized he was close to one of the small, open meadows in the woods.

There were faint noises of movement out there ahead, and once he thought he heard the sound of heavy breathing. He gripped the dog tightly and crouched where he was, listening. The sounds continued, and after a moment he realized that the herd of cattle must be bedded down for the night, there in the glade. The nearest ones were hardly more than fifty feet from him.

Andy had no wish to stir them up. On tiptoe, careful not to tread on a branch that might crackle, he started to circle the meadow, hauling the dog with him. But before he had gone a dozen yards, one of the cows got to her feet with a snort. At the same instant the boy heard a new sound—the voices of men approaching the seaward side of the glade!

One of them spoke a language Andy couldn't understand, but the other replied in a kind of broken English. "Beef!" he said. "You smell 'em, huh?"

A tiny light shone through the trees and grew more distinct. It was a lantern carried by one of the two men. He lifted it high above his head and its rays must have fallen on some of the cows, for he gave a quick exclamation of delight. His companion, Andy could now see, was carrying a musket. And both wore the scanty, bright-colored garb of tropical sailors.

CHAPTER XV

THE BOY STOOD rooted to the ground, not so much afraid as sickened by the thought of what he was going to see. In a moment these marauders would kill one of the cows—perhaps another Corson heifer.

Then a kind of reckless anger swept Andy. In a flash he knew what to do. The cattle were all up now and milling restlessly. It would take very little to stampede them. He let go of the collie and gave a push toward the herd.

"Sic 'em, Shep!" he breathed.

The big dog needed no second command. In one bound he left the shelter of the trees and dashed at the cows nearest him. They had no time to turn and face this new enemy. He was in among them, snarling and snapping at their legs. They tossed their horns and bellowed in fright. Then, so suddenly it took Andy's breath away, the stampede started. Straight across the meadow they raced, heads down, murderous as a charge of cavalry.

There was a scream of fear from the other side of the glade, and the musket went off with a loud report. But it was too late to stop the rush of maddened cattle. They swept over the place where the lantern had been and its light was no longer visible. In another few seconds, the whole herd had gone crashing away through the woods.

Shaken by the violence of the thing he had started, Andy stood there clutching his gun, wondering if the two men were dead. After a moment he heard a groan, followed by curses. Then another voice answered the first, and he felt better. He had saved the cattle, for the time being, at least. And whatever bruises the smugglers had received were well deserved. He looked around for Shep, but the collie must have gone off in pursuit of the fleeing cows.

Andy made his way westward, away from the beach, and when he had put enough distance between himself and the would-be cattle killers he headed north again. He had no doubt the sound of the musket shot would bring others from the beach, and it seemed a good idea to keep well to the other side of the island.

He wanted to get close to Townsend's Inlet if possible. From the high ground beyond the fish hawk's nest, he thought he might be able to see the smugglers' ship at her mooring and keep a lookout for Gillen's arrival. Also it would be a good vantage point from which to watch whatever might happen when the cutter got there.

At first Andy walked with the greatest caution. Not only was it difficult to see his way in the darkness but his recent encounter with the beef hunters made him wary. After a time, however, he began to move more boldly. The moon must have risen, for he found it easier to see the trees around him. He swung to his right and started up the slope toward the dune. Somewhere near he was sure to find the dead cedar with the nest in its top.

Just above him was a thicket of bayberry. He scrambled along beside it in the sand, looking for a break that would let him climb the rest of the way. And suddenly, right behind him, he heard a twig snap!

The boy whirled instinctively but the attack came too fast. A heavy body hit him and hurled him off his feet. The gun flew out of his hand. With his wind knocked out, dazed and gasping, he squirmed desperately under the weight that pinned him down. If he had been able to roll free he might have made it to the woods below. But his assailant was too quick for him, too strong. Fighting like a tiger, Andy smashed his fist into the face above him again and again. Then big hands had him by the throat, choking the life out of him. Pinwheels of light spun before his eyes and he seemed to be falling, faster and faster, into a bottomless black pit. He ceased to struggle as his last spark of consciousness flickered out.

* * *

The first thing Andy knew, when he came to again, was that his head throbbed and it hurt him to breathe. Then, when he tried to move, he realized that his hands were tied behind him. He was lying on his side in the sand. A few feet away figures moved in the glare of a fire. Gradually his memory came back and he recalled the night's events. Trying to reconstruct what had happened to him, he thought he must have been captured by one of the seamen from the smugglers' ship—perhaps the man set to watch over the signal light.

Nobody seemed to be paying any attention to him at the moment, and he had a wild idea of crawling off in the darkness and making his escape. But when he tried to roll over he found there was a rope binding his ankles.

There was a smell of roasting meat in the air. Some of the men around the fire were still gnawing on bones, and the boy knew they must have killed a cow or a calf. He wondered what had happened to Shep. The collie, he was sure, would have put up a battle before letting any stranger attack the herd, and it gave him a sick feeling to think of the old dog lying dead or wounded in the woods.

A big man in a blue coat and sea boots strode toward him and stooped to look into his face.

"Hey," he bellowed, "the boy's awake! You—Jose an' Miguel—come here!"

A couple of swarthy, half-naked sailors came up at the command. One of them grinned wickedly and fingered his long seaman's dirk. "We keel 'im now, eh?" he asked.

The mate, if that was what he was, shook his head impatiently. "Not yet," he growled. "Take him up to the inlet an' put him aboard the schooner. They ought to have the cargo unloaded by now. Throw him in the hold—down in the chains."

Andy was seized under the arms and hoisted to his

feet. The man who had been so eager to kill him saw the cord that tied his ankles together and swore in Spanish. With a flick of the knife he severed the rope and gave the boy a shove. "Queek, now," he ordered. "Walk!"

But before Andy could stumble more than half a dozen steps, the blue-coated man returned. "Hold on," he said gruffly. "Skipper wants to ask him some questions. Come here, you."

He grabbed Andy by the elbow and dragged him past the fire to a huge drift log that lay half-buried at the foot of the dune. A very fat, dark man was lolling there, bare feet stretched out in front of the log. He wore a scarlet shirt, open nearly to his waist, and there was a red kerchief around his head.

The man belched loudly and passed a brown hand across his drooping black mustache. His beady eyes looked Andy up and down. Finally he grunted something to the mate in a foreign tongue.

"He wants to know," said the fellow in the blue coat, "what you're doin' on the island."

Andy felt stupid enough, but he tried to look even more so. "Me?" he said. "I just come over here to fish."

The mate jerked his thumb to the log beside the captain, and Andy saw his own fowling piece lying there.

"Fishin'? With a gun? Don't lie to us, you brat!"

There was another question from the red-shirted skipper.

"Who else was with you?" asked the mate. "How many more?"

Andy licked his dry lips. For a moment he was tempted to tell them the island was crawling with armed men, but he knew it was no use. He shook his head.

"Nobody," he murmured. "I was all alone—just camping out."

The smugglers conferred for a moment. Apparently they decided there was nothing more they could learn from him, for the mate waved an arm and called the evil-looking pair of sailors.

"All right," he said. "Take him away."

As Jose and Miguel shoved him in front of them up the beach, Andy stole a glance seaward. The waning moon that was rising just before his capture had climbed higher in the sky. It made a dim path of silver on the waves. But the sail he hoped to find out there was not in sight.

The two men didn't seem to relish the job of escorting him. They grumbled from time to time and swore at him as they hustled him along. After more than a mile of walking they reached the curve of land at the mouth of the inlet. The tide was nearly at flood now, and waves were running so far up the beach that they had to go the last few hundred yards in the loose sand along the side of the dunes.

They were well to the westward now and nearing the quiet water inside the inlet. Ahead Andy saw the dark shape of a vessel riding at anchor. On the shore a man stood guard over a stack of bales and boxes, and just as they came up they heard a creak of oars. A boat was bringing more goods from the schooner. The rowers nosed her into the shallows and began carrying the cargo ashore and adding it to the pile already there. Miguel lent them a hand with the job while Jose watched their young prisoner. There was some palaver in Spanish, and at the end of it Andy was pushed into the boat. They took him out to the anchored schooner and, because his hands were still bound, they had to hoist him bodily up the side.

Standing there on the cluttered deck, the boy looked around him with desperate bitterness in his heart. The night sky and the cool south breeze had never meant so much to him as now, when he was about to lose them. He had no idea what his captors planned to do with him in the end. But it seemed a certainty that by this time tomorrow night he would be a long way from home.

There was a wild moment when he considered making a break for it—plunging over the side and trying to swim ashore. The risk of being shot or drowned was better, he thought, than the long-drawn misery he might face in the hold of the smugglers' ship.

But it was too late. As if he had read Andy's mind, Jose seized him by the arm and flung him down on the deck. Miguel laughed. He picked up a piece of rope which he whipped around Andy's ankles. The knot was jerked tight and the rope's end made fast to the cord that tied his wrists, so that his feet were drawn up behind him and he lay helpless.

"So, my leedle chicken," Jose chuckled, "you all feex' up, ready for roas'. Come, Miguel—we t'row 'im down below!"

They caught him by his neck and his knees and lowered him through the cargo hatch. Then the hands released their grip. He dropped the last ten feet into the black depths of the hold, landing with crushing impact on the chain ballast. Lying there bruised and shaken, he heard the hatch cover slam back into place above him.

For a long time he was too stunned by the fall to stir or think. Finally, with painful slowness, he moved his arms and legs as much as the tight cords would permit. It was hard to be sure because of the aches he felt, but it seemed to him that none of his bones were broken.

The hold, he found, was full of strange smells—strange, at least to a landsman like himself. Underlying them all was the stale, sickish odor of bilge water, but other, pleasanter smells were mingled with it. Tar and tobacco and spices had added their individual aromas. They stirred the boy's imagination with a hint of long voyages, distant ports and tropic islands.

There were noises, too. The timbers of the hull around him creaked gently as the ship rocked on the waves. He could hear the scurrying and gnawing of rats, and once a furry creature passed so close that it brushed his bare foot, sending a chill along his spine. He kicked convulsively against a link of anchor chain, and at the clanking sound the rat squeaked and ran away.

Faintly, from beyond the wooden walls of his dungeon, he heard voices. Someone was giving orders in harsh, guttural Spanish, and he wondered if it meant they were about to sail. But more time went by and the schooner still rode at her mooring. Gradually he felt the vessel swing sidewise, then come up with a tug against the cable. The tide must have turned. With high water the garvey would have been able to sail out across Stites Sound, and by now the schooner's hands were probably helping Gillen stow the smuggled goods aboard his craft.

Andy tried to figure what time it was. He knew the tide along the ocean was about two hours earlier than inland, on the shores of the Sound. If it had just passed the flood, here at the mouth of the inlet, that would make it now nearly four o'clock in the morning. He didn't know how long he had been unconscious after the fight on the dune, but it seemed certain that three or four hours had gone by since he was captured. In any case, dawn couldn't be very far away.

Dawn! How would he know, down here in the black hold? Day and night were both alike to a blind man, and he would lose all track of time. With a sinking feeling in his heart he accepted the bitter fact that his chances of rescue were growing dim. Something must have happened to Luke's signal fire or to the cutter. If all had gone as planned, the revenue vessel would surely have reached the inlet before this.

There came a bumping along the schooner's side and a sound of voices. Then feet trod the deck overhead. Andy heard the man in the blue jacket speaking.

"Come down to the cabin, Mr. Gillen," he was saying. "We can settle up for the cargo over a glass o' good wine."

The farmer's mumbled reply was indistinct, but the footsteps moved aft toward the companionway. Apparently the smuggler's invitation had been accepted.

CHAPTER XVI

ANDY LAY THERE for several minutes, straining his ears in an effort to hear more. But the sounds that came from the cabin were muffled by distance. Then he had an idea. While it was impossible for him to crawl, trussed up as he was, he could at least try rolling. He inched around till he lay crosswise of the ship and turned his body over toward the stern.

Each time he rolled it was an agonizing process. The huge iron links of chain dug into his ribs and scraped at his knees and elbows. But he was sure the voices in the cabin sounded clearer as he advanced, so he gritted his teeth and kept at it. Finally he passed the huge butt of the mainmast and reached a spot well aft, where the conversation came from almost directly above his head. The captain was talking and the mate interpreted his words into English.

"Pancho wants to know," said the mate, "why the last cargo didn't bring as much as the one before. He says it was a good cargo. There was the red silk—very fine—an' the cigars an' brandy."

Gillen's gruff voice answered. "Cigars—yes," he said. "Brandy—good. No trouble with any o' that stuff. It was the silk. Too showy. To sell it you have to put it out where folks'll see it, an' that got the drapers worried. First they didn't want to touch it at all. Finally I got old Fenimore to take it, but he wouldn't pay what it was worth. All I could get was sixty cents a yard."

When his words had been translated, the captain snarled something that must have been an oath. He rattled off several vehement sentences, and from the thumping sound Andy judged he must have pounded a fist on the cabin table.

"He says," the mate interpreted, "he thinks you're tryin' to cheat us. If he finds out you are, he'll cut off your ears an' nail 'em to the mainmast."

The threat must have had an effect on Gillen, for

when he replied he spoke in a more conciliatory tone.

"Aw, come now," he said. "Pancho knows I ain't really cheatin' him. We've been doin' business long enough to trust each other. Hm-m—don't mind if I do, thank'ee. That's first-rate wine."

He drank noisily, smacked his lips and then continued. "All I mean is, the silk's hard to get rid of, an' we both lose money on it. You take brandy, now. Handles easy an' brings a solid price—no questions asked. Or Madeira. There's a drink it seems like folks in Philadelphia can't ever get enough of. How 'bout a few barrels o' that, next trip?"

There was a consultation in Spanish between the two smugglers. Finally the mate spoke to Gillen again.

"All right," he said. "Pancho'll go along with you this time. No more silk, an' he'll try to pick up some Madeira. Now he wants to see the color o' your money. Count it out."

Andy heard the thud of a heavy bag on the table, then the steady clink of coins and the mumble of voices as they were counted. At length Gillen spoke up.

"Thirty-four hundred in gold," he said, "an' a thousand an' sixty in silver. The rest I had to take in paper money. Hard cash ain't easy to come by right now."

The man known as Pancho growled at that, and he and the mate argued with Gillen for several minutes over accepting the paper currency. At last they grudgingly agreed to take what he had brought them, and the stormy meeting wound up with another round of wine.

Just when Andy thought he would hear nothing more of interest the mate spoke up again. "By the way, Gillen," he remarked, "we caught a young lad tonight, snoopin' around on the island. He didn't seem to know much, an' I guess he just happened to be here. We've got him down in the hold now."

"What's his name?" asked Gillen quickly.

"Don't know. I didn't ask him. Why—you think he's dangerous?"

"He could be. What's he look like? How old is he?"

"Let's see," said the mate. "I'd judge he ain't over fifteen or sixteen. Sort o' tall for his age, but on the skinny side. Sandy hair an' freckles. He had a gun with him an' we've got it here. Want to take a look? Mebbe you'd reco'nize it."

Andy held his breath for he knew what they were about to find. At last he heard an explosive snort from Gillen.

"By thunder—look there!" the farmer exclaimed. "His name's scratched on the stock—Andrew Corson! I've had my eye on that young 'un for weeks. Been spyin' around my place—him an' his pious father. I reckon they suspicion somethin'. Give him to me! I'll take care of him!"

The frightened boy heard the mate speak in Spanish to the captain, who answered him. After an agonizing interval Gillen got his reply.

"Pancho don't like that idea," the mate reported. "You don't want more blood on your hands 'round here. If you kill him you'll get the whole countryside riled up. We'll see that the boy don't get home to tell any tales. Just leave him to us. Best thing is to put him ashore on one o' the dry keys, south o' Florida. That way he'll just drop out o' sight an' there'll be no trouble."

Andy heaved a shaky sigh of relief. At least he could look forward to a few more days of life. And if they marooned him on a desert island he might still have a chance of survival, however slim. He waited tensely for Gillen's answer. Apparently the farmer didn't care to make an issue of it, for he grunted something about hoping they'd do the job up brown—he never wanted to see the brat again. Then his chair was pushed back and he remarked that it was time to be going.

While the heavy footsteps moved out of the cabin and up to the deck, the boy started rolling painfully back to his original position. If Gillen changed his mind and demanded to see him he didn't want them to know he had been listening to all they said.

Before he regained the spot below the 'midships hatch he heard the boat shove off from the vessel's side. Then good-byes were shouted across the water, and in a few minutes the boat returned.

"All right, now—look alive there, lads!" the mate's voice called. "We'll have daylight 'fore you know it. Man the fore an' main halyards an' stand by to hoist sail. You, Manuel—Jose—Ramon—get the anchor up!"

There was a clank of pawls as the capstan turned and a squeal of cordage through the blocks, high overhead. The schooner gave a sort of shiver and heeled a little, so that Andy knew her canvas was beginning to catch the breeze. Soon the anchor left the water with a gurgling splash. He felt the ship come up into the wind, then settle away smartly on the starboard tack. She was running for the narrow channel that would take her out through the shoals beyond the inlet.

At that moment the hatch cover was pushed back and a rectangle of pale light appeared over Andy's head. He saw the snakelike end of a rope drop through. Then the sailor known as Miguel came sliding down it, holding on with one hand and his bare feet. In the other hand he was holding a pannikin of water.

When he reached the young prisoner's side he set the pannikin down and stood looking at him, scowling ferociously. Then he squatted and turned him over on his face. With rough dexterity he untied the cord that bound his wrists. It was all Andy could do to move his numb arms, but he managed to get them around in front of him and push himself up to a sitting position.

Miguel gestured toward the battered little pan of water and pulled a moldy-looking ship's biscuit from inside his shirt.

"Here," he grunted. "Eat."

Andy took the piece of hardtack in his stiff fingers and bit off a mouthful, then helped himself to a drink of water. Both were foul tasting but he knew he might as well get used to such fare. He was likely to have nothing better for a long time.

He had finished about half the biscuit when a sudden yell came from the deck above. There was a rush of bare feet on the planking and a rapid fire of orders, barked in Spanish. Miguel stared upward, listening, then leaped for the rope. He went up like a monkey, hand over hand, and disappeared through the open hatch.

Andy was too dazed for the next few seconds to do more than sit there, goggling at the brightening bit of sky above him. Then he knew what must have happened. The smugglers had sighted some kind of danger. Perhaps they were afraid of running on one of the shoals. Or perhaps—his heart beat faster—they had seen a sail!

The pounding chop of the channel against the ship's

sides gave way now to a different motion. He felt the slow roll and pitch of the ocean swell and knew they were outside. From the sound of the activity on deck he judged that added canvas was being spread—topsails, certainly, and an extra jib. The vessel heeled more sharply, confirming his idea.

In the midst of all the confusion above somebody must have remembered the open hatch. The cover banged shut and the boy was in darkness once more. But when he put out his hand he found that the rope was still dangling there.

Whatever was about to happen, Andy wanted to be free to move about. He felt for the cord at his ankles and began clumsily to untie the knot. It had been pulled so tight that his fingers slipped off the hard hemp again and again, but he kept at it in dogged desperation. At last he felt the bonds give a little. In another moment he had jerked them loose and his feet were free.

Boom! The sound of the cannon shot was unmistakable, even though it was muffled by distance. Andy had a prickly feeling in his scalp. The cutter had arrived in time!

Overhead the shot had caused excitement, too. He could hear Pancho's deep voice bawling orders and the rumble of guns being run out at the ports in the waist. In the dark of the night before he had seen carronades behind the bulwarks, though he had no time to count them. The schooner was well-armed and meant to make a fight of it.

There was a screaming sound as a shot passed overhead, and right on its heels came the jarring boom of the report. The boy shivered. Another one like that and he thought he might see daylight through the deck. Then he was conscious of a change in the schooner's movement. She was falling off the wind, swinging to the eastward. And in a few seconds he found out why.

"Ready a starboard broadside!" bellowed the mate. "As your guns bear—fire!"

The response of the carronades shook the schooner from deck to keel. They roared out raggedly—one, two, three, four—and the recoil threw Andy to his knees, half deafened by their thunder. He picked himself up, wondering and fearing what damage had been done to the cutter.

The answer came sooner than he expected. There was a crashing, rending noise, and again he was flung down on the chains. Screams of pain came from the deck. And even as he listened he became aware of another sound—the gurgle of water inside the hull. In the starboard side of the ship, not a dozen feet from where he lay, there was a gaping hole through the oaken planking. It was right on the water line, and at every downward plunge of the ship the green seas came gushing in.

Panic seized the boy then. He could hear masses of water sloshing beneath him in the hold below the chains. It could only be a matter of minutes before the inrushing flood crept upward to engulf him. The rats had heard it, too. They raced past him, squealing in terror, hunting for a means of escape.

Andy groped frantically for the rope. He had a wild notion of pulling himself up and trying to open the heavy hatch cover from beneath. Then his common sense returned. If the schooner was in trouble the battle would be ended all the sooner, and he could hope for release. He sat where he was, listening to the noises on deck. The screaming had stopped but he could still hear groans mingled with the shouted orders. The schooner came up sluggishly into the wind. That meant she was still in fighting condition, preparing to let go with her port broadside.

He waited for the overwhelming roar of it, biting his knuckles to stop the trembling that had come over him. But before the command could be given to fire there was another salvo from the cutter. This time there was no possibility of mistake. The smuggler's ship was hit, and hit hard. Her hull shook crazily and some part of her top hamper fell to the deck with a slithering smash.

The tumult that followed was indescribable. More of the crew must have been wounded, for their cries drowned out the orders the mate was trying to give.

One gun in the port battery went off with a thunderous report, but none of the others seemed to be in commission.

Gradually the bedlam quieted and there was a moment of near silence. Through it Andy heard a voice, faintly, as if from a distance. It was a voice he knew, even though it had shaken off its southern drawl, and he jumped with joy at the sound.

"Schooner ahoy!" it shouted. "Do you surrender?"

The boy waited breathlessly for the answer.

"No!" howled the blue-coated mate. "We'll fight as long as we're afloat!"

The words dashed all Andy's hopes. He collapsed on the rough iron of the chains and sobbed aloud. There was water over the links in many places now. It splashed against his skin, cold and relentless, an enemy that could not be held back. If the desperate crew of the schooner kept up the battle for another hour he knew he would die there, drowned like the squealing rats.

After a little he got control of himself. He clenched his fists and murmured a prayer. If he had to go he would try to meet his end like a man.

Each instant he expected to feel the crushing impact of another broadside from the cutter. She must have the smuggler practically at her mercy now, so why was the finishing blow delayed? While he waited, the uproar on the deck above him grew louder. Mixed with the outcries of the crew there was a new sound—the crackle of musketry fire—and the shouts rose to a howling crescendo.

At the height of the clamor Andy felt the ship lurch heavily and heard a crunching, scraping sound along her port side. Then, clear and sharp above the other noises, came a single voice like a bugle call. "Board her, lads! Take her, now! Give 'em cold steel!"

CHAPTER XVII

ANDY CLUNG to the hanging rope and listened to the fight that raged back and forth on the deck above him. His first reaction had been a surge of hope. Instead of sinking the schooner, Craig meant to capture her. But did he have enough men to overcome that vicious crew in hand-to-hand combat?

It was impossible to tell which way the battle was

going from the sounds overhead. The yells had given way to a hoarse, breathless panting, punctuated by the crack of pistols and the clang of cutlasses. Andy could endure the uncertainty no longer. With the strength of desperation he grasped the rope and climbed.

At the top he got a grip with his feet, so that one hand was free. There was a cleat on the underside of the hatch cover that give him purchase, and he pushed against it with all his might. Twice he tried without result. He knew he could not hang on much longer. With a final effort he strained at the cleat and felt the heavy wood move a little in its slides. There was an inch of daylight at one end!

The sight of it gave him renewed energy and he forced the cover back bit by bit. At last the gap was a foot wide—far enough open to allow his body to pass through. Gasping and nearly spent he hauled himself up, clinging by his fingers, till his head was above the level of the hatch coaming. Right beside him a wounded seaman lay groaning on the bloody deck but the main part of the battle had moved aft. Beyond the mainmast and up on the quarterdeck he could see a tangle of men locked in a life-and-death struggle.

He heaved his body upward through the hatch, picked up a boarding pike that had been dropped in the melee, and stumbled toward the fighters.

Less than a dozen men were still on their feet, and at

first glance the odds seemed to be about even. Craig had his back to the break of the poop and was swinging a marlinespike in his right hand, warding off the cutlass strokes of the blue-coated mate. The tall Marylander looked pale and spent, and there was blood on his left shirt sleeve.

As Andy reached the scene a lucky blow from the marlinespike knocked the sword out of the smuggler's hand and Craig lunged forward to strike him down. But at that instant the captain appeared behind him on the afterdeck. Puffing and streaming with sweat, the fat Spaniard would have been a ludicrous figure except for the wild gleam in his eyes and the pistol in his hand. He raised the weapon, aiming at Craig's head.

Andy had no time to think or plan. He hurled the pike like a javelin, point first at the scarlet shirt. It caught the captain in the shoulder. The pistol jerked upward as it was fired, and the fat man pitched to the deck below.

Craig meanwhile had knocked out the mate with a blow on the head, and with both their leaders down, the smugglers quickly lost their will to fight. When they had laid down their weapons the revenue officer looked around him and saw Andy for the first time.

"Great heavens, boy!" he panted. "What are you doing here?"

"I had a crazy idea I could see the whole thing from

the dunes," Andy admitted shamefacedly. "They caught me an' had me a prisoner, down below in the hold. It's a good thing you got here. I guess they planned to get rid o' me, from what they said."

One of the cutter's crew stood at his elbow. "That ain't all, chief," the man put in with a grin. "I reckon the lad saved your life. This fat pirate, here"—he nudged the red-shirted smuggler with his toe—"he had a pistol aimed at your head. Good thing the boy was handy with a pike or you'd ha' been a goner. Look, sir, you got pinked in the arm. Better let me look at the wound."

Craig laughed. "It's just a scratch—hardly bleeding now. Besides, we've got too much to do here."

He laid a big hand on Andy's shoulder. "Thanks, son," he said. "You're a good man in a fight." Then he turned to give orders to his men.

The shambles on the deck had to be cleaned up first. Two of the smugglers lay dead and there were half a dozen others badly hurt. None of the cutter's men had been killed, but five were bleeding from knife and gunshot wounds. The lieutenant hailed his own craft and had the surgeon brought over to look after the casualties. Then he turned his attention to the schooner itself.

"Get aloft there," he told the able-bodied members of his crew. "Repair that rigging so we can sail her into port. She's not much of a prize, but she'll be worth something to the government."

"Lieutenant," Andy put in timidly, "I don't think she'll sail far. There's a big hole down below an' she's taking water fast."

The officer went to the hatch and peered into the hold. "You're right about that," he replied grimly, and cupped his hands to shout across to the *Valiant*.

"Mr. Higgins!" he yelled. "Break out storm canvas from the sail locker and send it over here quick. We've got to patch her before she sinks."

In a few minutes the cutter's carpenter and two seamen had brought a square of folded canvas to the schooner's side and rigged a jury patch over the shot hole. Meanwhile four of the prisoners were put to work at the pumps. The rest, including the captain and mate, were herded into the forecastle under guard.

As soon as it appeared that the smuggling ship would stay above water, Craig gave orders to Ensign Higgins, his second in command, to sail her down to Cape May. Then he counted noses. Besides Higgins and the prize crew, there were six men left aboard the *Valiant*.

"You and I," Craig told Andy, "have got things to do ashore. Four men can handle the cutter in weather like this. That'll give us two to take with us. You, Matthews—Jones—get the dinghy ready. Bring your muskets."

He turned to the boy again. "Haven't had a chance to ask you," he said. "What happened? Did Gillen come out to get the cargo?"

"Yes," Andy answered. "He came aboard afterward an' paid 'em, too. I heard 'em counting out the money. There ought to be 'most five thousand dollars in the cabin."

Craig whistled. "That much?" he asked. "Come on, let's have a look. I'll have to take over her papers anyway."

The cabin of the schooner was small and untidy. Spilled wine and broken glass made the barefooted Andy hesitate before stepping inside. Under the captain's bunk there was a chest, closed by a heavy padlock.

"I reckon this is where he'd keep it," said the lieutenant. "But we've no time to fool around with keys."

He took an ax from a rack on the wall and smashed the lid with one well-directed blow. The money was there, and in a smaller compartment were the schooner's papers. Craig put the chest in Higgins' charge and returned to the deck, where the two seamen stood ready, holding the dinghy's painter.

Andy, meanwhile, had recovered his fowling piece from the cabin and followed Craig up the companionway. In a moment they were in the small boat, being rowed toward the beach. Looking at the shore the boy saw that the sea fight had taken place some three miles south of the inlet and they were now almost opposite the narrow part of the island, where he had crossed the night before.

"I've got my boat over yonder on the bay side," he told Craig. "We can take her right up the Sound. From our landing it's only a couple o' miles overland to Gillen's place."

They hauled the dinghy up the beach above the tide line and set out afoot for the other side of the island. As they went, the boy described his adventure from the start.

Craig chuckled when he heard how Andy and Shep had stampeded the cattle. "You must have given those smugglers quite a scare," he said. "What became o' the dog?"

"I don't know," Andy replied sadly. "All I hope is that he kept on following the herd. That way he might have stayed out o' trouble. For a while, there, I sure wished I'd had sense enough to do the same."

"You must have thought we were a mighty long time getting to the inlet," said Craig. "We saw the signal fire all right, but we were way north, up by the mouth o' Dennis Creek. Had to tack against the wind all the way down to the Cape. Listen—isn't that a dog barking?"

Andy heard it, too. It was the deep voice of old Shep, and it was drawing nearer. As they came out of the woods they saw the collie racing toward them. He leaped at the boy in such a frenzy of gladness that Andy was nearly knocked down.

"I bet you're hungry," Andy laughed. "So am I, but we'll have to wait a spell. Right now we've got more important things to do."

The tide was still fairly high on the inner side of the island, and they quickly launched the skiff.

"Maybe we'd better not use the sail," Andy told the revenue officer. "Gillen could see it across the marsh if he happened to be watching. He must have heard the cannon fire, but he doesn't know yet that we're headed his way."

Craig agreed. Jones and Matthews were lusty oarsmen, and they took the boat up across Great Sound at a good clip. It was about nine-thirty in the morning when they tied up at the Corsons' landing.

"If you need more men," the boy suggested, "I could run up an' get Jess an' Luke."

But the lieutenant decided against it. "The sooner we get there," he said, "the surer we'll be of catching him with the goods. I doubt if he'll put up much of a fight, an' we're strong enough to take him if he does. You'd better send the dog home, though."

Shep would have preferred to stay with Andy, but

he obeyed his master's command. Sorrowfully, tail drooping, he trotted off up the path to the farm.

"All right," said Craig. "Let's get our guns loaded and start."

Andy led the way along the edge of the marsh. A jutting point of land, overgrown with cedars, cut off their view of Gillen's dock. But when they had crossed it the boy stopped and pointed northward. Beyond a stretch of marsh and tidal creek they could see Stites Sound, and alongside the rickety pier lay Gillen's garvey. Even at the distance of a mile it was possible to distinguish a pair of moving figures, carrying bales and boxes to the farm wagon that stood at the shoreward end of the dock.

Craig rubbed his big, bony hands. "There they are, boys," he said with satisfaction. "We ought to be there in fifteen minutes. Let's go."

But it took longer than he had figured. There was an arm of the marsh and a deep creek extending for some distance inland, and they had to skirt it to stay on dry ground. A good half hour passed before they reached the boundary of the old Townsend farm.

"There's an old log barn right ahead here," said Andy, panting from the pace Craig had set. "That's where Gillen puts his smuggled stuff."

They went on more cautiously, with the boy in the lead. Through the cedars he could catch an occasional glimpse of the barn. At last he motioned to the others and halted, crouching, to peer out from behind a clump of brush. The log building was only a few hundred feet away and they had a clear view of its front and side. There was no activity around the place.

"Hm," said Craig. "Well, let's see what's here."

He went forward to the door of the barn. It had been repaired, Andy saw, and the big padlock was in place. In the sand there were fresh hoofprints and wagon tracks.

The lieutenant rubbed his chin and examined the heavy plank door. "We could break in," he said, "but it would take a little time. If he's storing goods here, they'll keep till later. Come on—it's the man we want now."

He strode off down the wagon track with the two seamen and the boy behind him. Suddenly, at the edge of the marsh, he stopped. They were in the open now, and the dock where the garvey lay moored was only a scant two hundred yards from where they stood.

Gillen had just climbed to the front of the loaded wagon and the Negro, Jim, was closing the tail gate. They saw the farmer look in their direction, then raise his whip and bring it down across the horses' rumps. The startled team leaped forward and the wagon went bouncing up the trail toward the farm.

"Blast it!" Craig exclaimed. "He saw us and he'll get away! Come on—after him!"

He led them across the rough, intervening ground at a run, but the horses were galloping now. Gradually the pursuers fell behind.

"Look!" Andy gasped. "He's not trying to get to the road! He's turned into the yard!"

It was true. The farmer had swung the frightened team to the right and pulled to a stop between the house and the heap of charred timbers that marked where the barn had stood. They saw him jump from the wagon and dash for the kitchen door.

"All right," said Craig grimly. "He won't go far now."

The winded men dropped from a run to a walk as they approached the buildings.

"Spread out," the lieutenant ordered. "Matthews an' Jones go 'round to the other side. Keep your guns ready and don't let him get away if he tries to make a break. The boy and I will stay back here."

As the two seamen moved to surround the house, Craig stepped forward toward the kitchen door. It was shut, and an ominous silence hung over the place. The tall lieutenant marched up the steps and knocked on the door with his pistol butt.

"Come out, Gillen," he commanded. "The game's up. Come out with your hands high."

For a moment they heard nothing. Then a gruff voice answered from inside.

"Git away from that door," Gillen growled. "Git away an' git off my property or I'll fill ye full o' lead. This here gun's loaded with solid ounce ball."

While Craig hesitated, Andy heard a movement behind them and whirled, raising his fowling piece. It was the old colored man. He stood there, unarmed, his knees shaking.

"Don' mess with that man," he moaned. "He mean what he say. He kill you sure, Mistuh. He's bad—crazy bad."

Craig stared at Jim for a moment, they slowly turned away from the door and came down the steps. He was frowning as he retreated to a safer distance.

"I've got no authority to break into a man's house," he said. "What we'll have to have is a warrant. You know how to reach the sheriff, Andy?"

"Yes," the boy replied.

"Well, get word to him about what's happened. Ask him to swear out a warrant an' get here as soon as he can. We'll stand guard till he comes."

CHAPTER XVIII

Andy was too excited to feel either hunger or weariness as he hurried down the road. Never in his life had he seen so much action crammed into a night and a day. But though his tired muscles reminded him he had had no sleep for thirty hours, he had no intention of missing any part of what might follow.

Running and walking by turns, he reached the Corson farm in twenty minutes. Luke was in the yard, playing with Shep, when the collie broke away from him and rushed to meet the younger boy.

"Andy!" cried Luke. "Hey, girls—he's home!"

Becky hurried out, followed by Elvira, and they were all talking and shouting at once.

"No time to tell you now," the boy panted in answer to their eager questions. "Get the colt saddled, Luke. I've got to ride for the sheriff."

His brother raced to the barn and Andy sat down to rest on the doorstep, handing his gun to Elvira.

"My goodness, Andy—you look like a reg'lar scare-crow!" Becky exclaimed. "Luke says you were going to the island. What happened? We heard shooting—big guns."

Andy nodded. "That was the cutter's broadside," he said. "They captured the smugglers' schooner after a big fight. I was aboard her—a prisoner."

"Oh, golly!" the girl whispered. "Honest? There's dried blood on your shirt. Did they hurt you?"

He grinned. "Hit me over the head, I guess. Any-how, I was out for a while an' when I came to they had me tied up. They were going to maroon me on a desert island, like Robinson Crusoe."

Becky's eyes grew bigger and bigger. "Wh—what about Gillen?" she asked. "Did the revenue ship catch him, too? Poor Prue's up in the attic, afraid to show her face."

"I reckon she won't have to worry," said the boy.

"Lieutenant Craig an' his men have got the house surrounded an' Gillen can't get away."

Luke returned with Starlight at that moment, and Andy heaved himself off the step. "Where's Jess?" he asked. "If you want to see the fun, you'd better round him up an' head for Gillen's farm. Craig's got Gillen barricaded in there, threatening to shoot anybody that comes close."

He climbed stiffly into the saddle and the black colt flew out of the dooryard like an arrow released from a bow. Almost before he knew it, Andy was pulling Starlight to a stop before the courthouse building in Middle Town.

He found Sheriff Leaming in his little office and told his story quickly. The big man nodded. He drew his hand deliberately across his drooping mustache before he pushed back his chair.

"How many men has Craig got?" he asked.

"Two seamen from the cutter. An' I reckon Luke an' Jess are headed that way."

"That ought to be enough," the sheriff remarked. "I won't wait to bring in deputies."

He took a printed blank from his desk and filled it in with painstaking care. When the warrant was made out at last, he rose ponderously, pocketed the paper and put on his hat.

"All right," he said. "My nag's out there at the hitch-rail, ready saddled. Let's be on our way."

Andy had to rein the colt in to accommodate his pace to the sheriff's. The county peace officer rode a big old plow horse, built to carry his weight, and it refused to move faster than a heavy-footed trot.

When they finally reached the lane leading to Gillen's farm it was evident that word of the affair had spread. Two wagons and half a dozen saddled horses were tied to fence rails along the lane. And around the premises, out of shotgun range of the house, several groups of neighbors were talking in huddles. They stirred as the sheriff appeared and started to crowd around him but he waved them off.

"Stay where you are, boys," he told them. "The County o' Cape May an' the U. S. Government are goin' to handle this."

Only Andy was allowed to approach the beleaguered house.

He tied Starlight to a cedar rail, well out of harm's way, and walked with the sheriff to Craig's side.

"Morning, Mr. Leaming," said the lieutenant. "We've got a little trouble here, and I wanted you on hand to make sure everything's legal. You brought the warrant, I reckon?"

The sheriff patted his pocket. "Got her right here. You goin' in?"

"Seems to be the only way," said Craig with a nod. "He's come to the end of his rope and he knows it."

The silence in the dooryard and under the trees grew heavy. Nobody moved. The farmers stood there leaning on their guns, watching the house, watching the tall Marylander. A horse shivered, jingling his harness, and as if the sound had broken a spell Craig strode toward the back door. He held an ax loosely in one hand. Otherwise he was unarmed.

A muffled yell came from inside the house. "I warned ye," Gillen screamed hoarsely. "Touch that door an' ye'll be a dead man!"

Craig's measured pace never slackened. He reached the top step, gripped the door latch and shook it. Then, cat-quick, he leaped sidewise as the blast of the gun shattered the oak panels. Even before the echoes of the report had died away he was on the steps again, swinging his ax. Once—twice—and the door crashed inward.

For a man of his bulk, the sheriff could move fast. He was right behind Craig when the lieutenant forced his way into the kitchen. Beyond them Andy could see Gillen struggling to reload the gun. But he was too late. They had him by the arms and they dragged him outside to stand on the steps, where Sheriff Leaming clapped a pair of handcuffs on him.

"You got all the evidence you need?" the county

officer asked Craig. "Or do you want to search the house?"

"I've got all I need. There's a thousand dollars' worth of goods in the wagon there, and I expect we'll find more in the log barn. I'll be obliged if you'll lock him up until I can arrange for trial in Philadelphia."

Mrs. Gillen had come to stand in the doorway, a shapeless, sagging figure, her hair hanging in strings, her eyes red with weeping.

"He didn't mean no harm," she quavered. "Beasley was allus a good, kind man. Look at the rings he give me—an' the silks an' satins! You can't put him in jail!"

The sheriff answered her, calmly polite. "Sorry, Mrs. Gillen," he said. "We can an' we will. Your husband's guilty of a crime against the Government, an' he's goin' to stand trial for it."

The group of farmers had gathered closer. Now from among them a voice spoke up. "You can hold him for more'n smuggling," it said. "He's guilty o' murder, too."

Andy stared at his brother Luke. The boy stood, white-faced but unflinching, with all eyes upon him.

The sheriff waited, choosing his words. "That's a pretty serious charge, Luke Corson," he said. "Whose murder?"

"The murder o' the man called Stumpy," Luke answered. "I can bring a witness to prove it."

Suddenly Gillen's wife changed from a poor, abused woman to a wildcat. "Yah!" she screamed. "It's that sneakin' hussy, Prudence! She's a low-down thief an' a liar, an' I'll whip the hide off her once I git her back!"

Sheriff Leaming eyed her coldly. "I don't think," he said, "that you'll ever get her back. Looks to me like you ain't a fit person to have charge of a young girl, an' that breaks the indenture. Come on, boys, the show's over. Let's all go home."

He borrowed one of the wagons that had been driven to the scene and started back to Middle Town with his prisoner. The others broke up into little groups and set off for home on horseback or afoot. Andy rode with Luke and Jess. He was beginning to feel the reaction now—so tired he could hardly give coherent answers to his brothers' questions. All he wanted was food and a bed.

Both were waiting for him when he got home to the farm. He ate the good, hot pancakes Elvira made for him, drank some milk and tumbled into the cot in his own little room. When he woke it was six o'clock and close to suppertime.

The kitchen presented a lively picture when they sat down to the evening meal. Mr. and Mrs. Corson were still at Cape Island, but there were six at the table including Prudence Mayhew. Andy was amazed at the change that had come over the bound girl. Her face, always so sad and pale, showed color and animation. She even laughed at the family's jokes and ate with a good appetite.

Most of the talk, naturally, was devoted to Andy's adventures. For the first time he had a chance to tell the whole story, and they sat for an hour, fascinated by his narrative.

"Say," he remarked, when he had finished, "there's one thing I haven't told anybody before, an' it may be important. The day Lt. Craig an' I went to the island we saw a man's foot track in the mud by that fresh-water spring. Not a boot, but a bare foot, good-sized, an' it looked as if it had just been made a few hours before. I wondered if Dode Gowdy might be hiding out over there."

"Well," Jess put in, "I'm—er—going down to the village tonight. If I should just happen to see Sheriff Leaming I'll mention it to him. I know he's still anxious to pick Gowdy up an' ask him some questions."

"If you should just happen to see him, eh?" Luke chuckled. "I don't know how you'll miss him, where you're going."

Jesse colored. "All right," he said. "That's where I'm going. But the sheriff leaves Faith an' me to ourselves most o' the time. If I do see him I'll find out whether he wants to talk to Prue, too."

He left a few minutes later, and he was hardly out

of sight when Sheriff Leaming himself rode into the yard. The big man was in a good humor. He joshed Andy about his activities as a revenue man and complimented the girls on the doughnuts and sweet cider they offered him. Then, more seriously, he turned to Luke.

"You said you had a witness to a murder," he told him. "I'd like to know more about it."

The boy glanced quickly at Prudence. "I–I don't know," he stammered, "whether——"

The fair-haired girl sat straight, her face pale but composed. "It's all right, Luke," she said. "I'm not afraid any more."

The sheriff looked at her kindly. "Let's see," he remarked, as if to put her at her ease, "you're the bound girl from Gillens', ain't you? Name of Prudence Mayhew?"

She nodded.

"I knew your father," Leaming continued. "A fine sailor he was, too. 'Twas a grief to all of us when he went down with his ship in that hurricane. Eighteen-eleven, wasn't it?"

The girl nodded again. "Yes," she said in a small voice. "And Mother died the same year."

"So," the sheriff went on, "you were indentured to Beasley Gillen an' his wife. How'd they treat you up there?"

"Not too bad, at first," she replied. "Most times I had enough to eat, and I didn't mind the work. It's only the last two or three years that—well, they changed. Mr. Gillen got hold of a lot of money. He began to drink more than he should, and he spent his cash on foolish things. They let the farm and the house go, but Mrs. Gillen had a lot of expensive clothes and jewelry. She was careless with them, too, and if she mislaid something, I was the one to blame. Then she'd beat me with a stick. Or she'd tell her husband and he'd take a horsewhip to me. It got worse this summer. Maybe Mr. Gillen's a little crazy—I don't know——"

Her voice faltered for a moment but Luke took her hand and she went on.

"The thing Luke wanted me to tell you happened about three weeks ago. It was the night before the news got around that Stumpy had disappeared. I was in bed and it must have been after midnight when I woke up. Mr. Gillen was running around in his stocking feet downstairs, and I heard him take his shotgun down from the rack over the mantel. He went out the back door then and shut it very quiet behind him.

"I went to the window and looked out but I couldn't see much in the dark. Then I heard a noise back by the barn. There was something moving out there and the chickens were cackling like they do when they're waked up. They quieted down after a minute or two.

I was just starting back to bed when I heard a gun go off."

The sheriff was leaning forward, looking at her intently. "Could you tell about where the shot came from?" he asked.

"Yes. It sounded as if it had been fired behind the barn, on the cart road that leads down to the landing."

"Then what happened?" Leaming asked. "Gillen came back in the house, I s'pose."

"No, not for quite a while. I guess it was half an hour anyway. And the queer thing was, he was still quiet about it. I thought he'd fired at a skunk or a fox or some other varmint. If he'd killed it he'd come back bragging. If it had got away he'd be angry, stamping around and cursing. But he tiptoed in as if he was afraid he'd be heard."

The sheriff frowned. "You're sure, now, Prue," he said. "You were still awake when he came back?"

"Yes. I couldn't get to sleep after I heard that shot. I just lay there listening and listening."

"All right. Go on," he told her.

"I always get up early," she went on. "I have to get the fire going, start breakfast and everything. Most times Mr. Gillen wouldn't be out of bed before seven o'clock. Old Jim did the chores. But that morning he was down ahead of me, even. He acted strange, walking back and forth as if he couldn't stay still. Sometimes he'd go to the door and listen, or he'd go to the window and look all around the yard, as if he thought somebody was out there. It scared me."

"Did he say anything—tell you what the shootin' was about?"

"No," she answered. "But when he looked at me it gave me the creeps. As if he wondered how much I knew and maybe meant to choke it out of me. When Mrs. Gillen came down she sent me out to gather eggs."

"Find anything out o' the way in the henhouse?"

She shook her head. "The door was shut, and all the hens were there. I counted, to be sure."

Sheriff Leaming stood up, scratching his head. "I believe you're telling the truth, Prudence," he said. "Maybe you'll have to tell it again—on the witness stand. I hope not. With what we've got on him, Gillen might own up to the whole thing.

"Anyhow," he told her with a smile, "you don't have to go back there to live. It's a shame you had to stand it as long's you did. You got anything at the Gillen house you need?"

Prue began to cry softly, but her tears were not unhappy ones. "No," she sobbed. "I never had anything but the clothes I've got on and one spare dress. I brought that with me."

"She can wear my things," Becky put in excitedly. " 'Course, she's older'n I am, but we're 'most the same size."

"All right," the sheriff laughed. "I guess you're in good hands. So I'll be gettin' along. Good night, all."

CHAPTER XIX

Leaming was out of the house before Andy remembered the information he had meant to give him. He ran after the big man and overtook him as he was untying his horse from the hitching post.

"Sheriff," said Andy, "I reckon I know where Dode Gowdy might ha' gone."

"You do, eh?" Leaming looked interested. "Whereabouts is that, son?"

Quickly Andy told him about the barefoot track on the island. "It was fresh," he said, "an' it was before the schooner came, so it wasn't one o' the smugglers made it."

The sheriff rubbed his chin. "Could be," he agreed. "A feller like Gowdy could live well enough over there—long as the weather stays warm, anyhow."

He chuckled. "Wonder what he thought of all the shootin' last night," he said. "Well, I'll take a couple o' deputies across there tomorrer an' see if we can pick him up. You want to go?"

"Gee!" Andy exclaimed. "Would you let me? I could take you over in our boat."

"Good idea," said Leaming. "You can look for us some time in the forenoon."

Andy didn't mention the project to his brothers and sisters until breakfast next morning. As he expected, Elvira was disapproving, Becky was wild to go with him, and the boys grumbled because he was getting out of picking apples for the second straight day. However, they admitted he couldn't back out if the county officers were depending on him for transportation.

"One thing, though," said Jesse. "You'd better get back here before supper. Don't forget Dad an' Mom'll be coming home. I don't know what they'll think of all your traipsing around."

"I'll do my best," Andy promised. He, too, had been

worried about what his mother would say when she heard of his recent activities.

He went out with the other boys to the orchard and helped with the apple-picking for an hour, keeping one eye on the road. When he saw the horsemen riding toward the farm from the direction of the village, he got off the ladder and ran back to the house to meet them. As they came into the yard he recognized Sheriff John Leaming and the two young deputies he had rounded up for the expedition.

"We're ready to start," the sheriff told him. "Might as well leave our horses down at the landin'."

Andy followed them down the path. As he came out of the cedars at the edge of the marsh he heard a quick patter of feet behind him and old Shep came racing to his side. The collie's tail was wagging ingratiatingly and he looked up into the boy's face with beseeching eyes.

The county officers dismounted and tied their horses to trees near the landing.

"I don't know 'bout takin' the dog," said Leaming. "Does he do a lot o' barkin'?"

"He'll keep quiet if I tell him," Andy replied. "An' he's got a pretty good nose, for a collie. I reckon he might be a help."

"Well," said the sheriff doubtfully, "bring him along, then, an' let's be goin'."

The tide was beginning to ebb but there was still water enough to let them sail a straight course across the Sound. As soon as Andy brought the boat to shore they hauled her out and paused to hold a council of war.

"There's two ways we could work on this," the sheriff told them. "One thing would be to start at the south end o' the island an' fan out, beatin' the woods an' brush all the way north to the inlet. That's a long, hard job, an' I'd rather try the other way first. We know there's only two or three springs where a man could get fresh water to drink. You found a track alongside one of 'em, Andy, an' I reckon if he's still here, he's left more tracks since then. We may be able to trail him. Anyhow, my idea is to work out in a circle from those water holes an' see what we find. Might as well start with the nearest one."

Andy had been standing close to the tide line, where the grass grew sparsely over the marsh mud. He looked down to see Shep sniffing at the soggy ground. A crab went scuttling away but the dog paid no attention to it. His nose was exploring a hollow, half filled with water. The boy crouched for a closer look and straightened up quickly.

"Sheriff," he called in a low voice. "See what you make o' this."

Leaming examined the depression and the fresh-turned mud beside it. "I'll be doggoned!" he ejaculated. "Somebody was diggin' clams this mornin'. Here's the stick he used!"

Andy pointed to a faint footprint in the grass. "Here, Shep," he commanded. "Follow him. Find him, boy—but keep your mouth shut!"

The old dog pricked up his ears, then dropped his head eagerly to the scent. He moved at an easy trot, straight up the path toward the woods, with the boy and the three men hurrying behind him. The trail he followed must have been fairly fresh for he didn't hesitate or cast about. They were in sight of the pond when Shep swung off to the right on an old cow trail that led southward through the cedar thickets.

They made their way in after him, pushing branches aside with their arms. In a few minutes they came out into a small clear space, and in the middle of it they saw the ashes of a wood fire. Andy ran forward. He put his hand in the little pile and found the ashes still warm. There was even a thread of smoke curling from a smoldering ember, buried underneath.

"Not more'n an hour old," the sheriff muttered. "Where'd he go from here?"

"I don't know," said Andy, "but this seems to be his regular cooking place. An' that looks like where he sleeps, over there."

At one side of the little glade was a heap of marsh

grass, matted down as if it had been used for a bed. Shep sniffed at it, then looked up at his master for instructions.

"That's right," said Andy. "Where is he? Go find him, boy!"

The dog searched back and forth across the patch of open ground, then seemed to gather enthusiasm as he picked up a fresh scent.

"By gum!" said the sheriff under his breath. "He's quite a dog. I'm glad we let him come."

Once more they had to move fast to follow the collie's progress. He led them southward again, then bore off to the left in the direction of the beach. In one place the trail crossed a swampy spot where highbush huckleberries grew, and Andy pointed to some of the branches which had been stripped bare of fruit.

He heard one of the deputies chuckle behind him. "Clams an' berries! How's that for a breakfast, Mose?"

"Reckon 'twouldn't stick to your ribs like fried ham an' 'taters," the other replied.

The sheriff held up his hand. "Sh!" he warned, and the talk stopped at once.

The dog led them straight to the low dune and would have gone on over if Andy hadn't held him by the ruff. Where they stood they were still hidden from the beach.

"Go ahead up, boy," Leaming whispered. "Take a look but keep out o' sight."

Andy crawled up the slope of sand till he could peer through the coarse fringe of grass at the top. The morning had been clear when they left the farm, but in the last few minutes it had clouded over. Now the boy saw a thick bank of fog creeping in from the sea. He could barely make out the white crests of the surf, fifty yards away. He hunched forward and looked up and down the empty beach. There was no trace of a human being to be seen. He turned back to the others and shook his head.

The sheriff wiped his forehead with a bandanna. "Well," he said, "I guess there's nothin' to do but keep on trailin' him."

"There's a fog coming in," Andy reported. "We won't be able to see much, but maybe Shep can find him. Go ahead boy—follow his tracks."

They scrambled over the dune as the dog led the way once more. Down on the level sand the trail swung to the right. The white blanket of mist had settled thickly over the beach and Andy had to quicken his pace to keep the waving plume of Shep's tail in sight. At this point they were only about a mile from the southern tip of the island. The boy wondered, as he hurried along, what errand the man they were tracking could have, so far down the beach.

Five minutes later he found out. The collie made a sudden turn toward the dune and lifted his head as if he was about to bark. Hastily Andy seized him by the long hair of his neck.

"No noise, Shep," he warned. "What's the matter? What's he doing?"

The sheriff, puffing at the rapid pace, had come up now. He looked inquiringly at Andy.

"I think he's there, just beyond the dune," the boy whispered. "Whatever he's up to, Shep doesn't like it. Look—his hackles are up." And he pointed to the stiff ridge of hair rising from the dog's shoulders.

They advanced cautiously to the dune with Andy still holding the collie in check. Then they heard the sudden bleating of a calf, startlingly loud in the fog-shrouded silence.

"Come on," growled Leaming, and he charged ahead over the crest of the dune. Released from Andy's grip, the dog flashed past him and disappeared in the mist. An instant later a snarling sound came out of the fog, followed by a man's cry of fear.

There was a thicket a few yards beyond the dune. Among the bushes they almost stumbled over the prostrate man with the big collie holding him pinned to the ground. Andy pulled Shep off and the tattered figure got shakily to its feet. He would hardly have recognized Dode Gowdy. The man's hair was long and unkempt, his beard shaggy and his clothing in rags. A few feet away a young calf lay struggling, its feet tied together with a piece of rope. And beside the calf was a long-bladed hunting knife.

"Well, Dode," grunted the sheriff. "Gettin' ready to do a little butcherin'?"

The man was still too frightened to answer. His eyes darted from the dog to the armed deputies, then back to the scowling sheriff.

"Take the rope off the calf," said Leaming, "an' tie this marsh-rat's hands behind him. He'll talk, 'fore we get him home."

They released the calf and bound Gowdy's wrists, then started back up the beach.

"We sort o' figgered you was hidin' over here," Sheriff Leaming told the prisoner. "You can tell me all about it now. Why did you burn Gillen's barn?"

Gowdy swallowed hard but made no reply.

"No use denyin' it," the sheriff continued casually. "We got all the proof we need. What I want to know is why."

At last the bearded man began to talk and the story poured out. "I set the fire," he said, "because Gillen's a murderin' devil. He shot my pardner, Stumpy, in the back. I was there an' I seen him do it."

"So?" asked the sheriff mildly. "How come he shot him?"

"Stumpy wanted to get some evidence Gillen was smugglin'," Gowdy replied. "Thought he could make Gillen pay him for keepin' quiet. I told him he was crazy but he wouldn't listen. Gillen heard him rummagin' around an' come out with a gun. I ducked out o' sight, but poor ol' Stumpy couldn't move fast enough. Afterward Gillen lugged him down to the landin' an' heaved his body over in deep water."

"Then all that huntin' for him was just a blind," Leaming remarked. "You knew all the time he was dead."

"Sure. I thought if you found the body with that gunshot wound, you'd hook it up to Gillen. When you didn't, I was mad enough to try an' get back at him myself."

"Sort o' foolish to run off afterwards, wasn't it?" the sheriff asked. "That made us pretty sure you'd had a hand in it."

The clam-digger had no answer ready. They had gone half a mile up the beach before he spoke again. "I seen the fight when they took that smuggler's schooner," he said. "Did Gillen get caught, too?"

"Gillen's where you're goin' to be mighty quick," Leaming replied. "He's in jail. If you help by tellin' what you know, he'll prob'ly be there for the rest of his life. An' you might get off a little on your sentence."

"Don't worry," Gowdy said grimly. "I'll be glad to talk."

They let Shep guide them through the fog that blanketed the island and found the boat without too much difficulty. The wind had died and it was necessary to use the oars on the way back to the mainland.

"I guess you know the waters 'round here better'n anybody else, Dode," the sheriff said. "These men o' mine can row. You tell Andy how to steer, so he can keep in the channel."

The marsh man had an uncanny sense of direction in the fog. Only once did the skiff run aground and then it was quickly pushed off the mud bank. A little after noon they made their landing at the foot of the Corson farm. The county officers took their prisoner away to the village and Andy and Shep went home.

CHAPTER XX

IT WAS AN EAGER GROUP of young people that waited that evening for the arrival of the wagon from the Cape. The boys had finished all the chores, washed up and changed into clean clothes. Elvira, with a little help from Becky and a lot from Prue, had prepared chicken and dumplings, sweet corn, yams, hot biscuits and luscious green apple pie. Now they sat on the grass by the door, eying the road anxiously. Prudence was the only one among them who was uncertain. She had had moments when she dreaded the coming of the elder Corsons.

Luke grinned at her reassuringly. "Don't you

worry," he told her, low-voiced so that the others wouldn't hear. "Mom always had a soft spot for you, an' Dad'll do as she says."

She was comforted a little, though she knew Luke himself was nervous. She had on a clean cotton print dress that was one of Becky's, and her hair, washed and neatly brushed, shone like gold in the sunset.

At last they heard the clop of hoofs and the light wagon came into sight. They could see Mrs. Corson waving from the seat beside her husband.

"Hurray!" yelled Becky, and she sped out to the road to meet them. When they drove in everybody started talking at once. Andy went to hold the horse's bridle, and big Jess hoisted his mother down over the wheel.

"My goodness!" she exclaimed. "You'd think I was light as a feather, the way you lift me 'round. How's everything? We had a wonderful time, but the best part of all is getting home!"

Suddenly, in all the commotion, her eyes fell on Prudence, standing still-faced in the background. Without a word she went to the girl and gathered her into her motherly arms.

"Honey," she said, "I know all about it, an' I'm so glad you're here. Jeremiah—come an' say hello to your new daughter!"

"You knew?" cried Luke. "How'd you know?"

His father chuckled quietly. "Stopped in the village an' talked to John Leaming," he said. "We heard quite a lot had happened while we were away."

He patted Prue's shoulder. "This child looks hungry, Mathilda," he said, with a twinkle in his eye. "An' for that matter, so'm I."

They all laughed and went in to supper. Andy, who had taken the horse to the barn, was the last to reach the table. As he entered a sudden silence fell and he knew they had been talking about him. He kept his eyes on the heaped plate before him and tried to eat. Just as the stillness began to grow uncomfortable he heard a stifled giggle from Becky's direction. Angrily he looked up.

His father was smiling. "Well, son," he said, "go ahead an' tell us the story. From all I hear it ought to be quite a yarn."

Andy gulped and stammered. "It was plumb foolishness that got me into it," he finally managed to say. "I hadn't any business on the island, an' I guess I deserved all I got. If I'd been strangled or shot or drowned it would ha' been my own fault, an' I didn't miss any of 'em by much. I'll tell you all that happened some time, but honest, I'd rather hear about what you did at the Cape."

"Yes, Mom," Luke put in helpfully. "Tell us who you saw. Did you get to go in bathing?"

"That I did," she replied with spirit. "Jeremiah rented me one o' those outlandish outfits an' I went right in up to my waist!"

She went on to give an account of the camp meetings, the big seafood dinners at the boardinghouse and the many old acquaintances they had seen.

Jeremiah Corson finished his pie and leaned back contentedly.

"I ran across a friend o' yours on the street, Andy," he said. "Lieutenant Craig, it was. He'd brought a schooner in to careen her an' patch up her bottom so he could sail her up to Philadelphia. He mentioned you might be interested."

The boy reddened. "Yes," he said. "Last time I saw her, I wasn't too sure she'd make it to the Cape."

They rose and the three girls started clearing the table. The boys and their father went out to enjoy the cool, pleasant dusk. The fog was gone now and a star or two was visible in the clear sky. The farmer asked a few questions about the apple-picking, then motioned to Andy, and they walked together out past the barn. The boy squared his shoulders. He expected a lecture and he knew he had it coming to him.

But there was no sternness in his father's voice when he began to talk.

"Son," he remarked, "according to Craig you handled yourself pretty well in that smuggling business.

He seems to think you were as much responsible as anybody for catching 'em. The cutter crew gets prize money for ships an' cargoes they capture, an' they've voted you a full share."

Andy's head was in a whirl. "G-gosh!" he breathed. "Honest?"

"Craig brought wagons up here Wednesday, while you were sleeping," his father continued. "They made quite a haul from that old barn. Four or five thousand dollars' worth o' liquor, cigars an' silk goods. Along with the money they found in the captain's locker an' the value o' the schooner, the lieutenant figures on a total of better'n twelve thousand. Around five hundred dollars o' that ought to come to you."

"Holy mackerel!" murmured the astonished boy. It was more than most farmers cleared in a year—enough, if he saved and added to it, to take him to the famous college at Princeton a year or two from now. That was a dream he had cherished for a long time and never dared to put in words.

They strolled on till they stood near the pole that supported the fish hawks' nest. One of the big birds was up there on the mass of sticks. Now the other came flying in across the twilight, its great wings beating with strong, slow strokes.

"Young hawks gone?" asked Jeremiah Corson.

Andy nodded. "Yes, they started flying a couple o'

weeks ago. They grow up fast. I reckon they're on their own now."

His father laid a comradely arm across his shoulders. "It's not just birds that grow up fast," he said. "Looks to me as if you'd done some growing up yourself this summer."

Andy smiled. "I guess maybe I have," he answered. "But if you an' Mom don't mind, I think I'd like to stay around the home nest a while longer."

www.ingramcontent.com/pod-product-compliance
Lightning Source LLC
Chambersburg PA
CBHW020552310726
48979CB00008B/1189/J